THE MUSIC MACHINE

by
Susan McAlpine

Marjorie L. Kelley, Ed.D.
Educational Designer

Sandra Speidel
Illustrator

Quercus Corporation
2405 Castro Valley Boulevard
Castro Valley, California 94546

Printed in the United States of America.
ISBN 0-912925-60-4

Contents

Rosa and Sue talk about Rosa's brother and the King High School Spring Show.

1

Brother Comes Home

"Hi Rosa!" Sue calls down the school hallway. Rosa Essay waits for her best friend by the door of their music class. Sue pushes her locker closed and runs to catch up with Rosa. Both girls are 17 years old. Next year will be their last at King High School.

"When is your brother coming to town?" Sue asks coming up to Rosa. "Do I get to meet him?"

"He's coming today," Rosa says. It's been a year since she's seen her brother, Ad, who lives in New York. Tonight is the King High School Spring Show. Rosa is going to be the star of the show and Ad will be here to see it.

"It's going to be the happiest day for me, Sue," says Rosa. "And yes, you can meet my brother. He'll be at the show tonight."

"How about the party after the show?" Sue asks. "Are you going to bring Ad?"

"You bet!" Rosa smiles, remembering how Ad is with a lot of people around. "Ad loves a good party. He has an apartment in New York now. He says it's one live party town up there in the north."

Sue begins to jive around in the hall. Rosa has been friends with Sue all year. She knows how high Sue gets when something important is about to happen.

"After next year we'll be through with high school forever," Sue says. "After that we can move to some bigger city and party all night."

"Sounds good to me," says Rosa. But she doesn't tell Sue that she has other ideas for her life. More students have come into the hall. They are waiting for Mr. Moe, the music teacher, to open the door.

"Mr. Moe says you'll be the hit of the show tonight," someone calls to Rosa. Rosa sees all the kids smile, showing they think so, too. She feels her face burn. Rosa wants her friends to think she sings well, but the thought of singing for other people makes her feel very shy. So far, only Mr. Moe has heard her sing. He thinks she's going to be a well-known star when she's older.

Just then Mr. Moe walks up. He's singing as he opens the classroom door. He always looks like he's up, Rosa thinks. If only she could be more like him.

"Rosa," Sue says as they go into class, "I suppose your brother's a great dancer."

Rosa smiles a big smile. "Listen, Sue, my brother has soul, but he's outrageous. All the girls keep away from Ad if they know what they're doing."

Two students in the front of the room turn around and look at Rosa and Sue.

"Stay with high school boys," Rosa says under her breath. "They aren't as dangerous!"

"Class has started," says Mr. Moe looking their way. He isn't smiling anymore. Rosa sees all of the class waiting for her and Sue to stop talking.

After school Rosa goes home to help May, her grandmother, around the house. Rosa lives with her grandmother who is very old now. Rosa has to do just about all the work around the house. That's why she can't be with her friends much. Rosa knows it was kind of May to take her in, as well as her brother, Ad, when they were children. Rosa loves her grandmother, but it's hard living with her because May doesn't like the way kids are these days.

Rosa's grandmother is always on her case about something. Ever since she was little, Rosa has had trouble keeping still when she feels mad. Now that Ad lives in New York, things have gotten bad for Rosa. Since he left home,

Rosa and May have had many big fights. Rosa tries to stop thinking about her grandmother while she's washing the dishes. She wants this day to be all good for her.

In only four hours the students, teachers and parents will hear Rosa sing. Best of all, her brother will be home from New York. Rosa feels warm from the sunlight coming in the windows. She sings her blues number as she works.

"I'm crying because my man is leaving me."

Rosa sings so loudly that she doesn't hear her grandmother come into the room. "My man comes no more, no more, no, no more."

"Rosa, what's that song you're singing?" Her grandmother sounds mad. All of a sudden Rosa drops a dish. She hears it crash just as her grandmother starts in on her again. "That isn't a song a good girl would sing!"

Rosa does not want to hear this. It's the song she's singing before the school tonight, but May doesn't know that. Rosa feels herself getting hot, but she doesn't want to let herself scream back at May.

"I'm sorry if what I say hurts you, May," Rosa says. "But why are you being so tight? I can't stand it anymore. I take responsibilities here at home, but I have no freedom. I can't see my friends or have clothes I like. I can't even sing my own songs. Singing is the only light in my life and now you want to take that away from me, too." Rosa feels tears start in her eyes. "Sometimes I can't help wanting to leave Burns and go live somewhere else far away from this town." *And from you,* Rosa thinks.

She sees that her grandmother is crying, too. She puts her arms around May and helps her sit down in a chair. May looks so much older right now. Rosa feels bad when this happens. But still, what she said about her life here is true.

"I guess you think being with Ad in New York City would be better than here?" her grandmother asks.

"Yes, I would like to be with Ad," Rosa tells her. "After all, he is my brother."

"You're just like your mother," her grandmother says, looking very sad. "Your mother thought her singing dreams would come true in the big city. She left home at 16 . . ."

Rosa has heard this story many times before. Then her grandmother says, "New York City is nothing but trouble."

"Ad likes it there," Rosa says. She thinks of Ad living in New York and driving a cab.

"But," her grandmother goes on, "he's had bad times. That boy used to get in so many fights. Then he had that run-in with the law. I guess that made him think . . . until next time he . . ."

9

Rosa sits back. May can go on and on, but halfway through her sentence she stops. Outside they hear a car pull up.

"Anyone home?" someone calls.

"It's Ad!" In a flash, Rosa is out the door and into her brother's arms. "Ad! Ad!" she says over and over.

"Hi, little sister," Ad laughs. He kisses Rosa, and now May is there, too.

"Ad, my boy," May says and starts to cry again.

Rosa thinks Ad looks so big . . . and so good-looking. He puts his arms around Rosa and his grandmother. They all go inside together. Ad says he could eat a house. May goes to get him some food and Rosa brings him a drink. Ad looks at Rosa, then he pushes up his glasses and looks at her again. He sees right away that something is wrong, but he knows now is not the time to talk. He gives her a secret smile and holds her hand tightly.

"So," he says, "the big show is tonight?"

Rosa smiles.

"You must be a real star," Ad laughs. "I hear one man has come all the way from New York to hear you sing!"

Now that Ad is home, Rosa is so happy she can hardly sit still. May comes into the room to bring some eggs.

"I forget what a beautiful sister I have," Ad says to their grandmother. "But I see it's true every time I come home."

"What song are you going to sing tonight?" May asks looking closely at Rosa.

"Oh, well," Rosa starts out. She feels her breathing stop. "Just one of the tunes Mr. Moe likes."

Ad looks at Rosa. Then he starts to eat and talk at the same time. Rosa has to laugh. She knows Ad is taking their grandmother's thoughts off of her. He's always been good at doing that.

"My little sister is going to be a woman soon," he says. "Only one more year at King High School, right?"

Rosa smiles.

"Well, May," Ad takes a long drink, "how about letting Rosa come live with me?"

Grandmother shakes her head.

"She will stay right here as long as I have my say!"

To Rosa this sounds like the last word. But Ad only laughs and falls down on his hands.

"Look Rosa! This is how we street dance in New York."

Rosa's eyes get big. Ad is really a good dancer! May looks like she doesn't feel so well. She takes the dishes out of the room. Ad jumps up. He opens the door and walks Rosa outside.

"Good-by, May," he calls out. "Rosa is taking me to see how much Burns has changed. We'll be back in time for her show."

Rosa looks back at the house. Their grandmother is standing at the window. Rosa waves. She feels free now that she is out with Ad, but Rosa thinks longingly of New York. Will she ever get to see it?

"Can you really sing?" Ad asks her.

"Yes, I guess so," Rosa says. "Mr. Moe, my music teacher, thinks I'm great. It was his idea for me to sing tonight. Not mine, I can tell you that!"

"What's the song?" her brother wants to know. "I guess this is a touchy question."

"A blues number Mother used to do," Rosa tells him. She sings some of it for Ad. He thinks for a long time. Then he says, "I remember! Sure, I remember that song now!"

Ad puts his arm around Rosa and takes her around and around. Rosa pulls away and dances off down the street. Only three more hours until she sings at the school.

2

Blues Baby

"Rosa, I'm really happy to see you!" Mr. Moe comes up to where Rosa is standing in the hall. "You're here before the others. That's good. Maybe you can do your song one last time for me."

"Sure," says Rosa. She thinks singing now might help her let go of the uptight feeling she has inside her. Rosa and Mr. Moe go into the classroom, and Rosa sings for him. When the song is over, Rosa asks Mr. Moe what he thinks.

"One word," says Mr. Moe.

"What's that?" Rosa wants to know.

"Explosive!"

Rosa feels her face burning.

"Tonight they'll drop dead when you sing, Rosa," Mr. Moe tells her.

Rosa pictures all the people falling over dead after she sings the blues. This makes her want to laugh, but then she remembers her troubles. Rosa thinks she had better tell him about her grandmother before the show.

"My grandmother and my brother will both be here tonight," she says.

"Great!" Mr. Moe was Ad's teacher before he left high school to move to New York. "It'll be good to see Ad after so long."

"You don't understand," Rosa cries out. "My grandmother doesn't like my singing. She's so out of it, I think she'll lock me away forever."

Mr. Moe makes a face at Rosa.

"She'll put you in a dark crevasse. People will pay money to see the girl who lives underground and sings the blues."

Now Rosa can't help laughing. She likes Mr. Moe for making things not so big and important. She knows what she said about her grandmother putting her away is stupid.

"It'll be OK," Mr. Moe says. "You'll see."

Now Sue comes into the room. One or two other kids put their heads in to wish Rosa well in the show. Next, another teacher comes to say it's time to get ready. Together Sue and Rosa go down the hall. They stop to look into the big, lighted room where the show will be. Rosa sees May and Ad sitting up close.

"Is that your brother, Rosa?" Sue says so no one can hear. "He's great-looking. And all the way from New York." Sue closes her eyes to think about this. "I'd like to go there someday."

"Me, too," says Rosa. "We could do what we want. No tight parents or teachers to push us around."

"When do we leave?" Sue asks. They laugh together. Then both girls fall quiet as they dream, thinking what this would be like. While they're standing in the hall, a teacher comes up.

"Rosa," she says. "The show starts in five minutes."

Sue goes to help Rosa get ready. After Rosa puts on her dress, Sue stands back looking at her friend. She has never seen Rosa so beautiful before!

"The boys will love you, Rosa," she says.

"But what about my grandmother?"

Sue thinks about how it is for Rosa. As long as they have been best friends, Sue has seen how Rosa tries to make her grandmother happy. Rosa can't have friends over, her clothes are never 'in,' and she has to work all the time at home.

Rosa and Sue stand listening to Mr. Moe open the show. He goes on and on about how great King High School is. Someone dances.

Then some boy reads a poem. At last it's Rosa's turn to sing.

Rosa goes out before her friends, their parents and the high school teachers. It's dark in the room now and she can't see Ad. She thinks she can feel her grandmother looking at her hard. Rosa's very shaky at first, but then the music starts. Her hand holds the mike and she hears herself sing. She opens up to her friends and finds she is no longer scared. When she's making music, everything is OK. The tight, sad feelings she keeps inside go away. Too soon her song ends. Everyone is screaming. Rosa's head starts to pound. The lights go on.

People come up to her. Everyone is pushing to get close to Rosa. Sue is there and so is Mr. Moe and Ad. All her friends want to talk to her. People she has never seen before tell her how great she was. Rosa feels shy, but she's also very happy. Now everyone knows she can really sing. She thinks about her grandmother who is not here. Where did she go? Is she very mad?

But Rosa forgets about that tonight. This is her night and if she can help it, nothing will get her down. There will be time for that tomorrow. The kids begin to talk about the party that's happening after the show. Just about everyone in the school is going to the party. Rosa takes Sue by the arm.

"Sue," Rosa says, moving toward Ad, "this is my brother."

"Hi," says Ad in a friendly way to Sue. "Are you a King High School girl who wants to grow up and come to the Big City, too?"

"I guess I am," Sue smiles.

Rosa gives Sue a push away from Ad and turns her aside. "I told you, Sue," she says. "Keep your eyes open. If you don't, you'll get burned!" Rosa knows this isn't true about Ad. But after so long she feels like keeping him to herself just now.

"What are you saying about me, little sister?" Ad calls. "Did you tell your friend that I'm from the wrong side of the tracks?"

Now Ad, Sue and Rosa all laugh. Other kids come up and together they go off to the party.

When Ad comes into the party with Rosa and Sue, he's as big a hit as Rosa. Rosa can sing, but Ad really lives in New York City. He did not just say he wanted to go there like the other kids. Ad went to New York, got a job and did not come back for a year. Ad is 18—not much older than Rosa's friends. But he comes across a lot older. He can do what he wants and he can live like he wants to, also. The kids have many questions for Ad.

"What's New York City like?" a boy asks him.

17

"Yes, Ad, tell us what it's *really* like," Sue says.

"Well," Ad thinks through each word. He's feeling very important around all these high school kids. "New York is very, very big. Big apartment houses, more people moving everywhere than in any other city in the world! There's any kind of food, drink or music. There's fighting over women, flashy cars and money. New York has it all . . . something for everyone!"

"Will you ever move back to Burns?" someone asks.

"No way!" Ad is sure of this. He feels as if it was ten years ago that he lived in this little town where nothing happens.

"Are you scared in New York?" a girl asks him.

"I shake day and night," Ad has a big smile. As everyone laughs, Ad takes Rosa's hand. He holds her close to him. Then he puts up his other hand to let everyone know he has something to say.

"My sister is coming to live with me," he tells the kids. "She's going to be the hottest star in New York someday."

The room is quiet.

The kids all look at Rosa now. "Are you really going to New York?" Sue asks what the rest of the kids want to know.

Rosa looks up at her brother.

"Oh come off it, Ad. When would I do it?"

"When school is over this year." He sounds so sure that Rosa feels her heart beat.

"What will May say?" she asks him.

"She'll say, 'Great!'" says Ad. "She'll say for me to get you out of here quick!"

"Sure, Ad." Rosa is mad. She thinks Ad is just being a show-off for all the kids. She thinks it's mean for him to get her going this way.

Sue turns to Ad. "If your grandmother doesn't let Rosa go to New York, you can take me."

"All right!" says Ad. Everyone laughs . . . but not Rosa.

The dancing starts again. Now Rosa is upset. She feels hurt that Ad could kid her about something like this. She wants the party to end. But if the party ends, it will be time to go home and face the music . . .

3

Facing the Music

"Ad, look!" says Rosa, taking Ad's hand. "It's so late, but May is waiting up for us!"

"Sure enough." Even Ad sounds a little scared.

It's 1:00 a.m. The party is over, and Ad and Rosa have walked home. They see that the lights are on in their grandmother's house. Rosa feels herself shaking all over.

"There's going to be big trouble, Ad." Rosa thinks they should turn around and go back. Seeing her grandmother through the window, Rosa stops dead in her tracks.

"Let's not go in, Ad!" she says. "Let's run away."

"I don't live here anymore, Rosa, remember? How can I run away? But don't be scared. We'll work out something. Come on." Ad wants to laugh at Rosa for being like a little kid.

Ad and Rosa go in the house. Their grand-mother is sitting by the door in her rocking chair. She looks like she's ready to attack them.

"Where have you two been so long?" she wants to know.

"At the party," Rosa tells her. The old woman turns to Ad.

"Rosa is a good girl when you aren't here, Ad," she says looking right at him. "What have you been drinking?"

"May," Ad says. He laughs right out loud. "This was a party at the school. I've been drinking soda all night!"

"May," Rosa says, feeling mad, "it's not always Ad getting me in trouble. I'm old enough to know what I'm doing."

"That's true," says Ad. "And Rosa is old enough to come live with me in New York when school is over. She can come back here for her last year at King High."

"No, Ad. I told you today not to ask me such a thing," says their grandmother. She closes her eyes and rocks, thinking of long ago. "I was an old woman by the time you kids come to me. Back then you looked so little and scared. You got off that train coming from New York and you cried out to me, 'May, May, we here. We come to live with our grandmother, May!' "

Their grandmother still has her eyes closed, but Rosa and Ad look down anyway. They remember the old days, too, and Rosa can't help feeling that somehow it must be wrong to want her own life so much.

They are all lost in the remembering. May says, "So I took you in when your own mother couldn't do nothing for you. I had you with me all them years after she was gone. I was old then and I'm older now. I guess you two going to pay me back this way. After all I done you leave me to die here all by myself."

Rosa doesn't think she can stand it anymore. But as she opens her eyes, she sees that Ad is looking right at May. He's thinking that this is the same old May. She's feeling sorry for herself so that Rosa will do what she wants. This time, Ad says to himself, she won't get away with it.

"Listen, May," he says in a slow way. "You heard Rosa sing tonight just like I did. I didn't dream she'd be that good, but she is. She sings beautifully. She's much better than Mother ever could have been. I think if she comes to New York and works hard, she can make it there. You got to let her, May. I'll take her with me for the summer. Then she can come back for her last year of school. I promise she will be OK."

Rosa, Ad and their grandmother are lost in the remembering.

Rosa has kept her eyes on Ad while he's talking. It makes her feel so good that he's trying to help her. But then she turns to May and her heart sinks. May's face is tight and hard as a rock.

"You're right, my boy, I sure did hear sister sing." Their grandmother says the words through closed teeth. Rosa wants to be somewhere else. She closes her eyes.

"What I think," May goes on, "is that good girls should not sing songs like that. And you are asking me to let sister go to New York with you and get money for doing it!" Now May is starting to scream. Both Ad and Rosa turn away from her. "And don't you think that I don't remember that song is one her mother used to sing."

"Talk to me! I'm right here," says Rosa.

"Your mother used to sing it for all them free-wheeling men she liked."

"Enough!" says Ad loudly. Even Ad is mad now, Rosa thinks. She hasn't seen Ad this mad for a long time.

Ad says, "Now I know that it's the right thing for Rosa to come with me, May. She needs to have some space . . . some time away from you. You could use time to yourself, too, I'll bet."

"I'll be the judge of that, Ad," May says. "Rosa is not going with you and that's the end of it."

Ad and Rosa stand together looking at their grandmother's back as she leaves the room. Rosa knows that Ad is used to winning people over, but this time he can't do it. Ad is thinking that he'll have two weeks to get May to give in. Then he will have to return to New York. He and Rosa go outside to cool off from the fight.

They don't say anything for a long time. Then Rosa starts to go in. "Thanks, Ad," she says. "You sure tried your best."

"I'm not through yet, little sister." Ad smiles.

Rosa puts her hand on his face. She says nothing. But she thinks, what a brother I have!

"Rosa," says Ad at last. "If May does not come around, what would you think of coming with me anyway?"

Rosa eyes Ad. "Leave May and run away from home? I never could do that!"

"Just an idea," says Ad. He shakes his head, running his hand across his face. "I'm starting to see things I'm so sleepy. Let's go in. We'll put our heads together in the morning and try to come up with something."

When Rosa is by herself in her room, she can't sleep at all. Today her feelings have been

25

up and down so much. She doesn't know if she should be happy or sad. Run away with Ad? How could she ever do that to May? But what about her singing? To Rosa making music is all there is in life. It's so important to her that there's nothing she wouldn't do to keep singing. But run away from her grandmother after all these years? After a long time, Rosa goes to sleep without any answers to her questions.

Two weeks pass. Throughout this time, Rosa listens to Ad and May fighting. Ad thinks of every reason in the world why May should let Rosa go to New York. But still May will not give in.

The day comes for Ad to leave. Rosa knows now that May is set on her staying in Burns. Rosa has thought a lot about running away. She feels bad about what it might do to May. But she has to live her own life if she wants to sing.

Ad gets his things together. No one says a word. Ad and May aren't talking. But when Ad phones for a cab, May comes over to him.

"I got to do what I think is best for sister," she says. Ad looks at his grandmother for a long time. Then he puts his hand on her arm and kisses her head.

"I know you do," he says. "But she would be OK with me. And I would have her back for school. You don't trust me, May. That's what hurts."

Rosa hears the cab. She runs out the door.

"I'm driving to the train station with Ad," Rosa calls to her grandmother. "I'll walk back."

Ad comes out after Rosa. He waves to his grandmother who's standing just inside the door of the house. Rosa opens the window of the cab. As it drives off, she calls loudly, "I love you, May." She can see by the smile on her grandmother's face that May has heard her.

Sitting back in the cab, Ad looks closely at Rosa. He sees by her face that something is happening, but he isn't in on it.

"Rosa?"

"Don't say a word, Ad, or I won't do it." Rosa falls back into the seat.

Burns is a small town and they are soon at the train station. Ad knows now that Rosa is running away from May. He doesn't say a word until they get out of the cab. Then he sees Sue. She's standing by Rosa's trunk.

"When . . . ?" Ad starts to say.

"Last night," Rosa tells him. "I left May a letter."

27

"Come on you two!" cries Sue. "I've been waiting forever. The train is leaving even if you aren't on it, you know!" Sue kisses Rosa and then Ad.

"If I come back," Ad calls to Sue from the train steps, "will I get another kiss?"

"Get out of here!" Sue laughs. "Have a great summer. Write me, Rosa."

Rosa and Ad sit at the train window and look out. They wave to Sue and call good-by one last time. The train starts to move.

Rosa pictures Sue, Mr. Moe, her school friends . . . and her grandmother. Then she pushes their faces away as if she were trying to close a book. In a flash, Burns is gone from sight. Rosa knows she'll be back in time for school, but she feels that a new life is waiting for her in the big city. Somehow things will never be the same again.

4

Rosa Makes a Move

Rosa doesn't think she has ever seen so many people in her life. In New York people are everywhere. She can't even get by on the sidewalk! Ad is walking far ahead. He looks back at her and laughs.

"Push, Rosa! You can get through," he calls.

Rosa feels so out of it from the trip that she can hardly walk. New York is really big. Ad and Rosa find a place to eat. Even in this restaurant, there are so many people. They find somewhere to sit, and Ad orders pizza and drinks. Then he looks at his sister.

"Listen to me," Ad says. "I know how it feels at first being in New York. And you're only 17. You can make it here if you want to. But you have to want to, Rosa. Don't let the big city get you down. You'll get used to it."

Rosa wants to tell Ad how much New York scares her. But it also makes her feel alive. The city is so dark, loud and closed-in feeling—

nothing at all like Burns. She looks at Ad, but she doesn't say any of this. Rosa thinks it's better to keep her feelings inside so she can work things out for herself.

"My apartment is up town," Ad says while he eats the pizza. "There are a lot of guys around there who like to cut up. Some get into trouble pushing drugs. There are also too many street women and robberies. But I got friends all over the place. I live on a good street because we know we can't get by without each other. We help each other out when we can. You'll be OK there, Rosa. My friends are your friends."

Hearing this, Rosa stops eating and looks right at Ad. Is this for real? Street women, drugs, robberies?

"If all that's true, I'm going back to Burns right now, Ad," she cries. "Why didn't you tell me before?"

Ad and Rosa stop eating. A man out on the street starts to scream. "That could be me," says Rosa. "That's just what I feel like doing."

"That's New York," Ad says.

All of a sudden they can no longer hold back what they are both thinking. For a girl of Rosa's background, Ad knows this is a lot to take in. Rosa asks herself what she was thinking of when she ran away. She knows full well it was her singing. But is it important enough so that she has to live in this kind of city?

Ad and Rosa think about the man and the scream and all that's been said. They look at each other and start to laugh. They laugh until it hurts. At last Rosa feels better about everything.

"It sure helps to laugh your troubles away," Ad says.

"It also helps to eat," Rosa takes the last of the pizza. "Can we have more pizza while you tell me some other great things about New York?"

"Sure," Ad orders more pizza and soda. He talks while Rosa eats.

"There's a guy I met at the races. His name is James White. He's the owner of a dance club up town called Street Scene. I called him from Burns to tell him about you. He wants to hear you sing at his club next week-end. That's when he tries out all his new people."

Rosa can't believe it. Can this be happening to her so soon? Maybe Ad is just putting her on to make her feel better. Ad knows what she's thinking.

"No," he tells her, "I'm not giving you a line. It's a fact, Rosa. And this place is really hot. It's your move now."

Rosa and Ad get their bags. They catch a bus going up town. Rosa looks out the window as the bus passes people—and more people. She sees so many contrasting faces. Will she ever stop comparing New York to little Burns?

Ad is the only one she knows here. Rosa holds on to her brother as if she's scared he'll float away from her. She feels shaky inside. She—Rosa—is going to sing in New York! No more high school shows for her. This town is the big time.

After a long bus ride, Ad and Rosa get off at Ad's street. Rosa sees that this part of New York where Ad lives is really run-down. They walk down the street. Rosa sees a man standing in a dark doorway. As they pass by, he says something that Rosa doesn't understand. Rosa feels herself tighten.

All of a sudden, Ad says, "There, Rosa, that's where I live!"

Across the street Rosa sees a high apartment house. "Looks great to me," she tells him. "But whatever happened to houses and green trees? New York is all apartments."

"And people!" Ad starts running as if he can't wait to get back. "Come on! There's one of those bad New York characters now."

"Catch!" someone calls out to Ad. He jumps into the air to bring down a frisbee. Rosa sees

32

that it was thrown by a boy sitting on the steps of Ad's apartment. His face is one big smile and he looks like he owns the place.

"Hi, Ad. Good to see you home, brother." The boy and Ad shake hands.

"What do you say, Mike?" Ad looks as if he has known Mike for a long time.

"Who's the baby with you?" asks Mike.

"This is my sister, Rosa," Ad laughs. "She's living with me for the summer while she tries to get into the music world." He turns to Rosa. "Meet Mike Match, Rosa. He's friend, basketball star and street fighter all in one." Rosa can see that Mike likes what Ad's saying about him. Ad puts his bag on the steps while he's talking. "You and Rosa are both 17, I think."

Mike eyes Rosa up and down. To him, she is like every other small town girl with big dreams. "In years only," Mike says. His smile is gone. The way Mike is looking at her makes Rosa want to be somewhere else.

"It's always good to see that New York is still here when I get home," Ad says. He sits down on the steps.

Mike throws his frisbee into the air. "What do you think will happen to it?"

To Mike, Rosa is like every other small town girl.

"I don't know." Ad sits back with a happy look on his face. "I guess with so many people all here together, someday New York might sink into the sea."

"Another great thought for the day, Ad." Rosa sits down beside her brother. She catches Mike's eye. She smiles at him, but Mike doesn't smile back.

"What makes you think you can make it here, baby?" Mike asks. "Every girl I know wants to sing or dance or be in plays. You got something they don't got?"

Before Rosa can answer, Ad says, "She's got a brother with friends in the right places. I got her a tryout this weekend at Street Scene."

For a moment Mike says nothing. He looks at Ad long and hard. Then he hits the frisbee on his leg and jumps off the steps.

"Man, I wouldn't let no sister of mine around that guy, James. He's all over women whenever he can be. And this baby doesn't look like she could take . . ."

"Back off, Mike," Rosa cuts in. She has had enough of this guy! "Just hold it a second. I may have a lot to learn in New York. But guys like you don't make it any better for me."

Mike turns away. Rosa can't believe she lost it like this. But then she sees a smile in Ad's eyes.

She feels better at once knowing that Ad likes the way she talked back to Mike. She and Ad look at Mike's back as he goes up the sidewalk.

"These girls are all the same," he says. "Big hot ideas! See you around, Ad."

"Sure, Mike," Ad calls after him.

"Don't let Mike shake you up," Ad says to Rosa. "He's always playing some game like that to show off. He's a great guy, but he's been real down this year. He's real good at sports. He was a high school basketball star until he left school. Now he just works . . . and fights."

Ad takes his bag and Rosa's trunk and heads up the steps to the door. Rosa stands up. She looks up the street to see if Mike is still in sight. "Well, I don't like him," she says. "Are all your friends like that?"

"He's one of the better ones," Ad laughs as they start up the stairs. Still, Rosa thinks that keeping away from Mike might not be a bad idea. She ran away from her grandmother's house to sing. She doesn't need some street fighter to bring her down, that's for sure!

5

Making Friends

The next morning Rosa gets up. She really *is* in New York City! Ad is sleeping after driving a cab all night. But he's left a letter for her. It says to go to the gas station at 120th Street West. This is where Mike Match works. Mike wants to show Rosa the ropes in the big city. She doesn't feel like going at all. But because Ad told her to, Rosa walks to 120th Street. She stands at the station looking around for Mike. She doesn't see him until she hears, "What can I do for you today, baby?"

Rosa turns around fast. It's Mike. He's looking at her in that way that turns her off.

"How about a soda?" he asks, holding out a can.

Rosa studies Mike with a cold look, but she takes the drink from him. She's willing to put up with him if he can help her meet some kids her own age. But she doesn't like having to talk to a guy who gets in fights. And she wants him to know it. Mike turns aside to put gas in a shiny red car.

"Flashy car," he says as he works.

Rosa thinks so, too. "Sure wish I had the money for one," she says longingly.

"When you get your name in lights, babe," Mike tells her, "you can have three like this one! If you don't make it, you'll just have to keep on walking like all the other dream girls around here."

"Drop dead!" Rosa asks herself how much longer she'll be able to stand this character.

Mike writes up a bill for the woman in the red car. Then he turns to Rosa. "What do you think of New York City?" he asks.

"Well," Rosa says, taking a long drink, "It's a hard town to get used to."

"You're right about that." Mike goes to help someone else. Soon he's back. "Do you sing as good as your brother says?"

Rosa starts at Mike's question. It's hard for her to talk about her singing to anyone. Even Ad. She doesn't know this boy at all, and she doesn't want to. Who does he think he is, asking such a thing anyway?

"Since you ask," she says tightly, "Yes, I'm good."

"You don't think much of yourself, do you?" Mike throws in. "And I guess you'll sing for me . . ."

"Like never," Rosa cuts him off. "But you can always pay to hear me at a club sometime." Rosa can't believe how she is with Mike. Talking to him makes her want to stand up for herself.

"I can't wait," Mike says in an off-hand way.

All at once, Rosa feels that she can't go on like this. She and Mike talk to each other as if they wish the other were dead. When next Mike looks at her, Rosa lets a slow smile pass across her face. I don't like Mike, she thinks. But I've got to make friends with him if he's going to be around.

"How's this, Mike," Rosa says, opening her hands as though they had a secret in them. "If you get me a flashy red car, I'll sing like a bird for you!"

Mike looks happy that Rosa has let up. "Sing first, then the car," he says.

"No way," Rosa comes back at him. "That game doesn't work with me."

They both laugh. Mike holds up his hands. "I give up! Here comes Bill. He takes over for me."

An older boy walks into the gas station. Mike waves at him.

"Now I'm off," Mike says. "Come on, baby. You can meet my friends now, but don't be put off by Willy. He's not as bad as people think."

Rosa and Mike go out into the street. Rosa feels better being with someone who knows New York—even if it has to be Mike Match. They go back to Ad's apartment house. Four kids are sitting on the steps. Everyone living on Ad's street meets here.

Mike and Rosa come up to the steps. A boy and two girls sit together talking. Below them is a tall hairy boy sitting off by himself. He doesn't look up. He's looking down at a rock that he's slowly pushing around with his foot. He has big bones. And it looks as though he couldn't hold his head up if he wanted to. To Rosa he looks like a big, dark, dangerous-looking bear.

Even after Rosa and Mike sit down, the bear-like boy keeps his face down. But the rest of the kids look at Rosa and smile. Mike stands on the top step. He holds up his hands as if he's about to give a speech.

"Everyone, meet Rosa Essay," he says loudly. "She's living here for the summer with Brother Ad. Like every other girl in New York, she wants to make it in the singing world. She's got a tryout for old hands-on James coming up at Street Scene. She's from Burns, Alabama and she needs friends. Anything else you need to know?"

"Sounds like you're reading a part from a bad play," one of the boys says.

"I am," Mike waves his hand at Rosa. "And here's the star . . . until she falls out of the sky!"

Rosa feels her face get hot. Thanks a lot, Mike, she thinks. What did I ever do to you? But she tries to smile at the other kids. They tell her their names—Luther, Jill and Harriet. Like Rosa, they will all be going back to school at the end of summer. Also like Rosa, it will be their last year of school. She knows right away she'll like the girls. And Luther, who has his arm around Jill, looks OK, too. But the big boy sitting below still hasn't said a word. As if Mike had read Rosa's thoughts, he kicks Luther's basketball down at the bear-like boy.

"Willy," Mike calls down to the boy. "What's the trouble? Turn around and say hi to this beautiful baby I found at the gas station."

Willy's head comes up very slowly. It's clear that he isn't happy about being talked to. He gives Rosa the once over but says nothing. In a minute he goes back to pushing the rock.

"Willy don't like girls much," Luther tells Rosa, "but I melt when I see them." He opens his arms. "Want to come into my warm, friendly . . ."

"Cut it out!" Jill kicks Luther. "You're taken, remember?"

"Oh, rats. I forget, Jill." Luther looks down smiling. "You're so mean to me."

Sitting on the steps in the sunlight, Rosa feels good about being with these kids. She laughs at the way Jill and Luther talk to each other. Then she looks over at Mike making circles with his finger on the steps. Everyone is happy just to sit and say little. Rosa has never talked much around her friends, anyway. So it feels a little like being at home.

"I remember coming here when I was only 14," Harriet says, turning to Rosa.

"Where did you live before?" Rosa wants to know.

"In the southern mountains," Harriet tells her with a smile. "We're both from the South."

"But you don't talk like it," Rosa says.

"I didn't want people asking me all the time where I come from." Harriet looks right at Rosa to see if she understands.

Rosa doesn't want to let these kids know she's scared of New York. But she is secretly happy that Harriet can understand what's going on with her. She's feeling better every minute until Luther says, making up a new name for her,

"Say, Southern, sing us some hot number, will you?"

Rosa feels a flash of cold go through her. Very, very slowly, Willy has moved around on the steps until he's facing Rosa head on. Rosa's eyes get big. She's never had anyone look at her this way. She feels like she's in danger, but she knows it's not true. By now, all the kids have turned toward Willy.

"I want to hear you, too," Willy says. When he talks, he sounds as cold as ice. "But I know you little southern girls are uptight as . . ."

"That's it, Willy. Cool it right now, man." Mike is up off the steps in a flash. He takes up the basketball and runs down the sidewalk with it. Then he circles around and throws it up to Luther.

"Good catch, boy," he calls out. Then, "Come on, Willy. Let's get the court before those guys from 140th Street beat us to it."

Willy doesn't move, but Luther jumps down where Mike is. They pass the ball and throw it at the wall as if there were a basket. Rosa is shaking, but she holds her hands together tightly so no one will see. If only Willy would go away with his mean talk and his scary face! But Rosa can't help feeling good about Mike helping her out. She doesn't think she'll ever

43

like him much. But she feels better about him now.

Willy sits with a dark look in his eyes. After a time, Jill gets up and walks down the steps by Willy. But as she passes him, he puts out his foot, tripping her. Jill catches herself in time and then turns on Willy.

"You! You're nothing but a no good, Willy," she spits out. "You find trouble every place you go. No one wants you around here but Mike, you hear me? And Mike just feels sorry for you!"

Rosa sees Willy jump up and stand facing Jill. His hands are tight and he looks like he's going to blast off any second.

"Out of my life, girl," he says slowly.

"I'll stay out of your life, Willy," says Jill steaming. "But you and your dope keep out of mine."

Now Mike is up on the steps again, pushing Willy down toward the street. "Get lost, Jill!" Mike calls loudly as if he really means it.

Before Mike can stop him, Willy gets a can on the sidewalk. He throws it at Jill. She moves fast, and Willy sees the can crash through a window.

"You're asking for it!" screams Willy. He turns and tears down the street. Rosa sees that he runs to one side as if something is wrong with his legs. A man runs out of the apartment house.

"Who did that?" he wants to know. Then he sees Willy going up the street. "That kid again? This time I'm calling the cops."

"Oh, man, don't be so tight with him," Mike says, standing on top of the stairs. "You know the cops took him in just last week."

The man eyes Mike. Then he looks at the smashed window. "Some friends you've got, Mike. Going to hand over the money for this window?"

"If that's the way you want it, man." Mike pulls out a few bills and hands the money to the man. "How about the rest next week?" he asks. The man takes the money and gives Mike a hard look. Then he goes in the apartment house.

"Fast thinking, Mike." Luther hits him in the arm. "But how long can you take the fall for Willy?"

"Listen," Mike says. He looks around to see if anyone but his friends is listening. He moves closer to Luther. "Willy goes to court next week. They got him for dope about six weeks ago. If they don't let him off this time, he'll get thrown out of the halfway house he's been living in."

Rosa looks at Mike. Her eyes are big. All of a sudden she sees that these city kids live a very different life from her friends in Burns.

"Now he's clean," Mike says. "And that's really hard for him." He turns to Jill. "So get off his back, Jill. Willy doesn't need that kind of talk at all. You know his trouble got really bad when he played around with dope. But he doesn't need for you to tell him about it."

"Sorry, Mike." Jill feels bad. "I didn't think. I just can't stand that guy. But I know he's your best friend."

"It's OK. I'll forget it . . . this time."

Luther takes the basketball from Mike. "Who wants to play ball around here? Don't all jump up at once now!" Luther looks at Rosa. "You play, Southern?"

"I play," Rosa says with a smile.

"Good," Luther turns to Mike. "And how about you, my good man? We need a leader."

Mike makes a sound in his throat. "You know I'm not too happy about girls on the court, brother. But it's your game, I guess."

"Come out of the dark, man." Luther laughs and throws Mike the ball. "Lead the way. Come on, Harriet and Jill. Show us what you can do."

They head off down the street. Mike and Rosa fall back from the others.

"What do you think about Willy?" Mike asks Rosa.

"I've never been around anyone like that before," Rosa tells Mike. "Is he really a good friend of yours?"

"Yes, we've been friends since we were little kids." Mike looks off as if he's remembering. "We've come through a lot together, Willy and me. Like the time we were climbing in the park and some rocks nailed his leg. He's not really so bad if you know him like I do. He's just real mixed-up. Now he's in hot water because he got into dope. I'm trying to find a way to help him kick it."

"How can you do that?" Rosa wants to know as they get to the basketball court.

"Come on, you two," Luther takes the ball from Mike and runs ahead.

"I don't know," Mike says slowly. Then he stops. He and Rosa look at each other. Rosa isn't used to boys like this. She wants to drop her eyes, but she keeps looking at Mike. At last he asks, "Why don't you like me, Rosa?"

Rosa plays with a tear in her t-shirt. Why is he asking her this? Can't he leave her be?

"I do," she says, not yet believing her own words. "But you can give people a really hard time, Mike."

"You mean like Willy does?" Mike asks.

"No, not like Willy!" Rosa is sure of herself this time. "You two are not alike to me."

"Let me get a foot in the door, baby," he says. Mike makes a circle with his hand on top of Rosa's head. "You might find I'm not such a bad guy after all."

Mike runs onto the court. He leaves Rosa standing on the sidewalk, thinking. A foot in the door? Is this guy for real? How can he think she could ever like him that way? Her singing is what's important to her, not some street guy who has friends on dope!

"Rosa, come out of your day dreams and get on this court!" Mike calls out.

"That is your leader talking," Luther says. He runs by Jill and takes the ball from her. Now Luther throws to Mike as Rosa runs on the court. Mike cuts by Rosa and puts the basketball in her hands.

"Play ball, baby!" he says loudly. Rosa throws it up in the air.

"Basket!" Mike calls.

6

Don't Let Us Down

"A lake in New York City? Come off it," Rosa says. She's waiting for Mike to get off work. He's going to show her a part of the city where there aren't so many people. Rosa can't wait to see this.

"I tell you, there is a lake," Mike calls out to Rosa after giving a man at the gas station his change. "Want to bet on it? Come with me and I'll show you. We'll get a boat and float around looking at the birds and listening to the airplanes. How about that?"

Rosa looks at Mike as if he had two heads. "You like to do that kind of thing?"

"Why not?" Mike says as if it's something he does all the time. But then he says, "It'll be our secret, OK, babe? Luther and Willy would never let me live it down. Well, what do you say, Rosa?"

"I don't know . . ."

"Come on, beautiful. You'll have a great time."

At last Rosa tells Mike she'll go with him. She can't be gone too long because she has to meet Ad at a restaurant up town. James, the owner of Street Scene, will be with Ad. He'll see Rosa for the first time.

When Mike can leave, they catch a bus to West 75th Street and walk through the park. Mike doesn't talk much. Rosa knows that he must think a lot about Willy. No one but Mike has seen Willy since he broke the window.

Rosa is thinking so hard about Willy that she starts when Mike cuts into her thoughts. "When are you going back to Burns?" he asks her.

Rosa has a flash of her grandmother's face. "I don't know," she says. She's asked herself the same question many times. "I ran away."

Now it's Mike's turn to jump. "You what?"

Rosa looks down. She doesn't answer right away. Then she says slowly, "I ran away. Ad's train was leaving and all I had to do was get on and go. So I did . . ."

"That's a trip." Mike sees Rosa in a new light. "I thought you were the kind of girl who never broke rules."

"I do follow rules," Rosa says at last. "I've always been good—too good. Now I have to live my own life if I want to keep singing. Do you think I like the idea that I ran away? I left my grandmother to get by on her own."

Rosa turns away from Mike and stands still under a tree. So this is New York—this is the town her own mother left home for. For a minute Rosa can't help but wish Mike weren't with her. She knows she would sing. She would push the sad feelings out through the music. This has always been her secret way. Mike and Rosa look at one another. When he played basketball, Mike let his own hurt out on the court. Now all he has is fighting. Rosa and Mike aren't really so different at all.

"Now, where is this lake, anyway?"

"Right before your eyes, baby!" Mike waves his arm.

Rosa looks up. She can't believe it. There really is a big lake down the field from them. Mike and Rosa go out on the lake. Mike lets the boat go and closes his eyes. Rosa looks out at the trees around the lake and listens to the sounds. It's the first time since she's been in New York that she hasn't heard cars.

She looks at Mike, sitting back in the boat with his feet up. He sure is good-looking, she thinks. Out loud, she asks, "Why did you want to do this?"

"To make believe I'm not in the city." Mike moves his head. "When I'm here, my troubles melt away. What do you think? Sounds like a song . . ."

Rosa pictures Mike in the city. He is so different on the street. She knows she's seeing a side of him that he doesn't show anyone else. Mike opens his eyes. He sees Rosa looking at him. Rosa's face burns and she turns away.

"I'll bet you're thinking about the old woman you live with," he says. "She wouldn't go for a guy like me at all."

"Don't call her an old woman—even if she is."

"OK. OK. I'm sorry. It's just the way I talk. Are you mad at me, Rosa?" Mike puts his hand in the water and looks away.

"No." Rosa smiles. "I could try to be mad, but I don't think it would work."

"Good!" Mike throws water on her.

"Cut it out!" she cries.

"All right. Let's get this thing back so you can go meet Ad and old James." Mike sits up in the boat. "I'll go up there with you. I haven't seen James for a few weeks. Remember what I told you, baby. Don't let James get too close to you. Put him in his place from the start."

Mike and Rosa leave the boat and walk back through the park. She feels very close to Mike right now. Rosa talks about her singing. And she finds out that Mike has a dream of his own. He tells her that someday he would like to be a teacher.

They get the bus to the restaurant where they're meeting Ad and James. It's dark inside the restaurant, and people are pushed together. At last Rosa sees Ad. With him is a small older man with a big head. His hair is shiny and pushed down, and he has big teeth. The man keeps moving his hands even when he's sitting down.

"Rosa, you made it!" Ad says, looking up. "Come over here and meet James."

"Hi, kid," says James. He and Rosa shake hands. Then James and Mike shake. "How goes it, Mike?" James asks. He and Mike are old friends.

"OK," Mike sits down. Ad orders more drinks.

"What cuts with Willy boy these days?" asks James. "I heard the law is on him. Is he in a bad head trip?"

Rosa looks at James. He sure has a different way of putting things.

"I don't know," Mike says. "It's his thing."

James turns back to Rosa. He likes to clean his teeth while he's talking. Rosa looks away.

53

"So," James puts his hand down on Rosa's arm. "You sing for me in six days, right, kid?" Rosa tries to smile. "Big Ad here," James goes on, "wants you to be a hit. You will not let him down now, will you? Are you willing to do whatever it takes to make it?"

Rosa remembers what Mike has told her about James. If she makes it through the tryout, this man will be her boss! She looks at Ad and says strongly to James, "No, I can't let my brother down." But inside she feels scared.

James pushes his face close to Rosa's. "Look, Big Eyes, lots of birds come around wanting to sing for me. Are you so much better than all the others like your brother says?"

"Yes, I am," Rosa has trouble getting the words out. She wants James to move over, but he gets even closer to her. Who is this guy anyway? Why does Ad want her to sing for a man like this? Well, Rosa thinks to herself, I guess putting up with guys like James is what it takes to make it big. It's really now or never. If I can't learn to step around some stupid guy like James, I might just as well go home.

Rosa listens to Ad, Mike and James talk. They go on and on about what's happening in their part of New York. The talk turns to Willy once again. Mike says that he and Luther are after some guys who want money from Willy. There's going to be a big fight, Mike tells James. Can James get them a car? Rosa doesn't think she can take much more. She turns away from the others and looks at people coming into the restaurant.

All of a sudden, Rosa feels a hand running up her back! At first she thinks this can't be for real. Ad, Mike and James are all talking. No one is looking at her. But no, it's true. And she knows it's James' hand. Rosa stands up, kicking over her chair. James jumps.

"What's wrong?" Ad asks. He eyes Rosa.

"Nothing!" Rosa knows she sounds too loud. "I'll be right back." She leaves the room to cool off. When she comes back, Mike walks up to her. She sees that Ad and James are not within hearing.

"What's up?" Mike asks. "Is it James?"

Rosa can't say anything because she thinks she might cry. Mike knows what's going on, anyway.

"Get it together, Rosa," he says, taking her back to the others. "Play it real cool. I'll get him out of here and you and Ad can talk about it."

When Mike and Rosa return, James rocks back in his chair and looks up at Rosa. "I'm going to have some friends come around to hear you, kid. What do you say to that? You're not uptight about anything, are you?"

Rosa sits down. She takes her drink and runs her finger around the top of the glass. Slowly she looks at Mike. Any minute she knows she might let James know what she thinks. And then he would never let her sing at his club. James and Ad are both looking at her, waiting for her to answer. To Rosa it feels like years pass before Mike stands up.

"Let's get moving, James," he says.

"OK," James gets up, too. "Come on over to my place. I'll see what I can do to help with that little trouble you and Luther are having."

Everyone shakes hands and says good-by. Mike and James walk away. At the door Mike turns and waves. Rosa and Ad sit in the restaurant drinking. Ad slowly takes off his glasses and starts to clean them. When he's through, he puts them back on and looks at Rosa.

"Well," he says. "What did James do that got to you so much?"

Rosa gives Ad the story. She can see that Ad is not at all happy about this.

"I know James is all over the girls," Ad says, "but not my sister. If that guy touches you again, so help me . . ."

Rosa feels good having Ad stand up for her this way . . . but what about her singing? "I can't stand James," Rosa throws out. "But Ad, I want to sing. Mike says I have to learn to get by men like James."

"How does Mike know about this?" Ad asks.

"He could tell," Rosa says. "That's why he got James out of here."

"Rosa." Ad takes Rosa's hand in his. "This is all in a day's work for James. Girls come and go at his place all the time. If you can get by him, you'll do OK anywhere."

"Trust me, Ad," Rosa says. Even if the thought of being with James is so scary, she's just got to sing!

"I do trust you," Ad says warmly. "It's James I don't trust. I don't want you to get hurt."

"You're not going to get in my way, are you, Ad?"

"No," he says at last. "But I hope I'm not sorry. I tell you I feel like I could cream James."

"I'll be OK." Rosa sounds so sure out loud.

"Time to go," Ad says. "I have to work now. My cab is outside. I'll take you home in it, OK?"

"Great!" says Rosa. She's never had a ride in a cab before.

"It'll be a fast trip." Ad stands up. "You take your life in your hands." He pays for their drinks and moves Rosa through the people to the door.

"Ad, you aren't going to get into that fight with Mike and Luther, are you?"

"No way," Ad says. "I'm through with street fighting."

They walk down the sidewalk and get in the cab. Rosa is starting to feel scared. An hour ago she sounded so ready to take on the world. Now that she's thinking about James, the tryout, Mike, the fighting and Willy, she isn't so sure of herself. Things race by as the cab screams down the street.

7

The Killing

Rosa's tryout at Street Scene is in two days. She's really scared now. Ad tries to make her feel better by getting Chinese food for them to eat one night.

"Rosa?" Ad puts the food on dishes. "You'll be all right. You'll be better than all right. You'll sing great! Just don't get so uptight."

"But I've had bad dreams," Rosa tells him. "Sometimes I'm not even able to sleep. One night I dreamed I tried to sing and no words came out. Then James came after me with a gun."

"It's OK," says Ad. "It was only a dream. Now eat up!"

"Ad, food isn't going to help me," Rosa says, pushing it away from her. "I can't eat this much all the time. I've put on 10 pounds in New York."

"You haven't eaten anything," Ad says. He puts more food down. Then he takes out some money and hands Rosa $100. "Get a new dress for the tryout. That will make you feel better."

Rosa looks at the money she's holding in her hand. She's never had this much money before . . . and all for clothes! Rosa knows Ad doesn't have much money. He must have saved for weeks to have this much all at once.

"Ad," Rosa says, throwing her arms around him. "I can't believe it. No one has a brother like you!"

"So true, Rosa, so true."

After they eat, Rosa goes with Jill to babysit. Jill can't believe how much money Ad gave Rosa.

"Will you come with me to get the dress?" Rosa asks her new friend.

"Sure," says Jill. "Say, Rosa, what's the story with Mike?"

"What about him?" asks Rosa. But she knows her face is burning.

"Do you still believe your own line that he's not your boyfriend?" Jill wants to know. "You two seem really tight to me."

Rosa knows it's true. While Ad works and sleeps, Rosa is sometimes with other kids. But she's happiest with Mike. The more they're together, the better they understand each other. But each time they part, Rosa gets her head together. It's then that she thinks she will forget him. She has to. She wants to think only about singing.

"Jill," Rosa says, "I really don't want a boyfriend. Mike's just a friend. I ran away from my grandmother to come to New York to sing. That's what's important to me right now. I just can't let anyone take me away from my singing."

"Right! I can dig that," Jill tells Rosa. But she says it as if she isn't sure she believes what Rosa is saying. "But you also need to have a good time while you're in New York. And Mike is a good guy for that."

All of a sudden, the girls hear the scream of cop cars in the street below. The sounds are close enough to be in the room.

"Come on," says Jill. "That's on this street!"

With the baby in her arms, Jill runs down the stairs. Rosa follows her outside. Cop cars line the street. Cops are everywhere, running around with their guns out. And there are newspaper photographers trying to get a story. Rosa and Jill see Mike and Luther. They can tell that something very bad has happened. Mike and Luther come over.

"Big trouble," Luther says. "Someone who works at Street Scene got killed near here. The cops say the hit was for James, not the guy who got it." Then he sees how scared Rosa looks. "It'll be OK, Southern. There's a lot of guys who can't stand James."

Rosa starts. What did Luther mean by that? Does this have something to do with Ad? Could the cops be looking for her brother? He was sure mad at James, but she knows Ad would never kill anyone! Rosa wants to ask what has happened, but she can't get the words out.

Mike and Luther look mad and scared at the same time. Mike stands close to Rosa saying nothing. A cop brushes by them and runs into the apartment. Then another one pushes right up to them.

"Well, have you thought about it?" the cop asks Mike.

"I tell you I don't know where he is." Mike backs away from the cop. "What is this—a shakedown? You can't book me for not knowing something."

"Right you are," the cop blasts back. "That is, if you really don't know!"

Rosa feels her head hurt. She thinks she might fall. It is Ad they want! What if they find out she's Ad's sister and hold her until Ad turns himself in?

"Mike," she says. Mike looks at Rosa and sees that she isn't well. He puts his arm around her and turns back to the cop.

"Who's she?" the cop wants to know.

"Mike, get me out of here," screams Rosa without thinking.

"What's going on here?" The cop comes close to Rosa.

Mike is looking hard at Rosa. He doesn't understand what is wrong with her. Now Rosa feels the eyes of everyone. She wants to get away from all the faces.

"Maybe you better come with me to the car," the cop says to Rosa. "I'll bet you know something I don't."

"Let me talk to her," Mike says. "She's new in town."

"I don't like this at all." The cop is mad now. "You have three minutes, Mike."

Mike takes Rosa into the apartment house away from all the people. Jill and Luther follow them in. Rosa is shaking all over.

"What's with you?" Mike asks. "You can't get these guys going, Rosa, or you'll be in hot water."

"They're looking for my brother, aren't they?" says Rosa with a tight throat.

"Your brother?" Mike starts to laugh. "Now I see what's going on. No, Rosa, you're all wet. They aren't looking for Ad at all."

Rosa puts her hands over her face and turns away from the others.

"Rosa . . . ?" Mike touches her back.

"I'm sorry I'm such a baby," Rosa says, crying into her hands. "I thought it was Ad and . . ."

"I hear what you're saying, beautiful," Mike tells her. "It's OK."

The cop comes back in from the street. He looks at Rosa and Mike.

"Well?"

"It's OK," Mike tells him. "This is Ad's kid sister. She thought you were looking for Ad."

"Ad!" the cop laughs. "He's clean as far as I know." Then to Rosa, "Do you know something I don't?"

Rosa shakes her head. The cop turns back to Mike. "Now," he says, "are you going to help us out or not?"

"I tell you, I don't know where Willy is!" he cries. Mike looks like he can't take much more. "Anyway, you said the fingerprints on the gun don't match his."

"That's right," the cop says slowly. He looks as if he would like the fingerprints to be Willy's.

"Then why do you want him at all?" Luther asks.

"Well, Mr. Know-it-all," the cop spits out. "We just want to talk to him." He turns back to Mike. "As for you, don't go anywhere. We'll want you if there's a change in this case. And one more thing. I heard some talk about a street fight." The cop eyes Mike, and then Luther. "You boys wouldn't know about that, would you?" Luther and Mike say nothing. "That's what I thought," the cop says. He walks out the door. Rosa looks at Mike.

"Will you tell me what in the world this is all about?" Rosa asks loudly.

Luther can see that it's hard for Mike to tell Rosa, so he says, "Willy went to Street Scene to ask James for money. James wouldn't come through, so they got in a big fight. Everyone heard about it. When this other guy was killed, the cops went after Willy. They know he didn't do it, but you know cops. They got to have someone to pin it on."

"Then where is Willy, Mike?" Rosa asks.

"I don't know." Mike hits his hand into the door. "Ask Willy."

"Who else would know if you don't?" Jill says.

"Get off my back," Mike cries. He turns and heads out into the street. Rosa, Jill and Luther stand together after Mike goes. No one feels like talking. The baby Jill is holding starts to cry.

"I better take this little guy back," says Jill. "Are you coming, Rosa?"

Rosa thinks she wants to go home and wait for Ad. On the steps of Ad's apartment, Rosa sees both Ad and Mike sitting together talking. She can't hear what they are saying, but she knows it's about Willy. Rosa doesn't want them to have to stop talking. She goes in the apartment by the side door.

How sad for Willy, Rosa thinks to herself. He must be really scared with the cops after him. She sits down by the window. In Burns, Rosa heard about kids who got in trouble, but she didn't know them. She thinks about how hard it must be to have a friend in trouble. Rosa opens the window. It's a hot night. She pictures Willy running. She pictures Mike thinking about his friend. And she starts to sing the blues.

8

The Tryout

Right now Rosa and Jill are in Ad's apartment listening to his tapes. Today is the big day! At 2:00 p.m. Rosa will sing for James at his club, Street Scene. Rosa has her new dress ready to take with her. Ad says she looks really good in it. Besides looking great, he thinks she'll sing well today. But Rosa feels as if something is going to go wrong. She doesn't feel good about herself. But she also knows she had better if she wants to sing well.

Rosa has mixed feelings about this tryout. As the day has gotten closer, she has thought more and more about May. If she can make it singing, she knows she'll move away from Burns after high school. Maybe it would be better for her grandmother if Rosa tripped up at Street Scene. Then she would have to go back to Burns. Besides thoughts of her grandmother, there's James. The thought of seeing him again makes Rosa want to throw up. She knows she has to make it clear to him what kind of girl she is. She has to be sure he understands that she

67

will sing for him, and that's all she'll do. Besides thinking about the tryout, Rosa has also taken the time to listen to Mike. He's been with Rosa a lot and she knows he needs her to talk to about Willy. Where has Willy gone? No one has seen him, even Mike, since the night of the killing. The cops have said they'll track him down. It's all Mike can do to keep it together himself.

While Rosa sits thinking about all of this, Jill brushes her hair. Rosa loves talking to Jill about boys, music, school . . . . They are getting to be really great friends. Rosa wants to try on the new dress one last time. Jill helps her into it. While they are talking, there's a sound outside the door.

"Who is it?" Rosa asks loudly.

"Letter for Rosa Essay!"

Jill opens the door. In walk Mike and Luther.

"Hi, girls!" Luther falls down at Jill's feet with his arms out. "Oh, where have you been, love of my life?"

"Luther!" Jill holds back a smile. "Stop being so stupid and get up!"

"Come on, baby, why so touchy?" Mike asks. Then he sees Rosa standing in the next room in her new dress.

"Rosa, you look icy! What's happening around here? What's the big secret?" Mike sits on a chair arm. "You girls can let us in on it, can't you? Come on . . ."

Rosa and Jill look at each other. Luther lets his head fall on Jill. "Tell me the secret, oh, beautiful one. If you don't, I will take you away to my dark and dangerous desert cave!"

Jill pushes Luther. "Will you cut it out, Luther! Someday I'll go mad around you."

"I got it!" Mike jumps up. "Are you singing today at Street Scene, Rosa?"

"Good guess, Mike," Jill throws out. "Now get lost. Rosa doesn't want to be around people today."

Mike pushes Jill out of his way. "What does that make you, Jill? A chimp?"

"It's true, Mike," Rosa says. "I only want Jill here. I'm really scared."

"Rosa," says Mike, standing so close to her, she can feel his warmth. "You'll do OK."

Rosa smiles. "Thanks, Mike, but can you go now? We'll see you guys tonight after the tryout, OK?"

"We'll have a party." Luther walks to the door. "So put on a happy face, Jill, my girl. Come on, Mike. Let's hit the streets. Maybe we can find some guys to beat up."

"Luther!" Jill cries as Luther goes out the door. "You better stay out of trouble if you want me around for long!"

Mike is still standing by Rosa. He runs his hand down her arm. "See you," he says. Then he turns to Jill. "Let up on Luther, Jill, or he may just find another baby to love!"

"Get out of here, Mike!" Jill says in a cold way.

Mike goes out the door, but comes back in a minute. "I can't forget this." He holds a letter out to Rosa. "It came for you downstairs, Rosa."

Rosa takes the letter from Mike. After he goes, she sinks into a chair and opens it. It's from Mr. Moe, her music teacher. He tells her that her grandmother has a heart condition. Because her constitution is strong, the doctor says she may live another year or two.

Rosa drops the letter. A part of her feels like crying. But a bigger part of her feels like ripping up the letter. Now I'm going to sing, Rosa thinks. But did I have to hear this news about May right before going on? Thanks a lot, Mr. Moe!

Jill has been looking at Rosa. "What's wrong?" she asks. "Is the letter from home?"

Rosa starts, remembering where she is. "Yes, it's about my grandmother. My music coach writes that she has a bad heart. He says she can't live more than a few years at the most."

"I'm sorry, Rosa," Jill says. "I know how you feel. My dad was hit by a motorcycle when I was 12. He was hurt real bad, but he lived for two more years. It was hard knowing he would be gone soon."

Rosa and Jill sit thinking. The sunlight streams into the room. Jill remembers her father, and Rosa pictures her own world without her grandmother in it. May . . . At this moment Rosa forgets the bad things about her grandmother. All she can think of is big, warm May who loves her and Ad. All of a sudden Rosa is crying. The tears run down her face. She shakes all over from thinking about how she would feel if May died. Jill puts her arms around Rosa and they hold each other. Each is trying to push her sad feelings inside. They don't hear Ad come up the stairs until he's just about in the room. When his key turns in the door, Rosa runs over to the tape player.

"Jill, listen," Rosa says. She turns up the music so Ad will not hear what she has to say. "Don't tell Ad or anyone about my grandmother until the tryout is over, OK?"

"OK," Jill says loudly over the sound of the music. Ad walks in the room. Rosa knows her eyes must be red, and so she runs out to wash her face.

"Hi, Jill," Ad says, throwing his newspaper on the chair. "Rosa, are you ready? We don't

71

want to be late for the tryout."

"I'm just changing out of my dress," Rosa calls back to him.

"Now that Ad is here, I'll get going," Jill says loudly through the door. "Call me when you get back from the tryout, Rosa." She walks out. Rosa comes into the room, holding her new dress in a bag.

"That was fast." Ad looks at the closed door. "Jill didn't even say hi!"

"You know how Jill can be." Rosa sees the letter from Mr. Moe by the chair.

"Well, she can forget my vote!" Ad goes in the other room. Rosa pushes the letter under the chair with her foot just as Ad comes back in. He stands looking at Rosa while he brushes his teeth.

"You look like you're keeping a cat in the bag, Rosa. What's up?"

"I am!" Rosa cries, jumping out of the chair. "Let's get this over with."

Ad laughs as they go into the hallway. "If you sing good at Street Scene," he tells her, "it will not be over with. It'll just be starting."

"That's what raises my hair on end," Rosa says. Then before Ad can say any more, Rosa goes down the stairs two at a time. "You think

72

you're a real fast guy, Ad. Let's race to the bus stop. I bet I'll win."

Ad calls down, "This is a kid's game, Rosa." But he is down the stairs after her and heading for the street. As soon as he hits the sidewalk, Ad throws back his head. He walks slow and cool again.

Street Scene is closed when Rosa and Ad get there, but James lets them in. The sight of him makes Rosa's insides turn over. She goes to put on her new dress. While she's gone, Ad and James talk about the guy from Street Scene who got killed. They know the cops want Willy, but they know he didn't do the killing. After Ad and James talk, Rosa and her brother have to wait a long time. There are other girls singing at the tryout, too. Rosa finds it very hard to sit listening to these different girls sing. She can't stop thinking about the letter from Mr. Moe.

Again she pictures her grandmother. This time she sees May in the old rocking chair by the door. Her grandmother can be very trying, but Rosa knows that May has had a hard life. She thinks about May taking in her and Ad when they were children. It was not something May ever dreamed would happen. I sure didn't help, Rosa says to herself, by running away just like mother did. Rosa doesn't hear the band stop playing. She jumps when Ad shakes her.

"Come out of your dream, little sister. It's

your turn next!"

It's very dark inside the club. Many people are sitting close together. They're all friends of James, and they're all drinking highballs. Rosa walks up the ramp toward James. He looks at her for a long, hard moment. Then he says so no one hears, "Here we have another small town girl who sees her star shine in the east. Don't be scared, Big Eyes. Each of us has had a wish smashed sometime."

"I've never made a wish in my life," says Rosa evenly. "Just play the music, James."

James and Rosa look at each other. Rosa can tell that James doesn't like women. She knows he likes to see them do badly at the tryout. It makes him laugh because he knows how much they want to make it. James is waiting for me to fall on my face, Rosa thinks to herself. This is the real test. I've got to start somewhere. And if I can sing for James, I can do it anywhere.

At last James turns away from her. He waves a hand for the band to start. Then he gives Rosa a mike and shows her how to use it. Next he tells her how to stand, move and turn while she sings.

Rosa listens to everything James says, but she doesn't feel well at all. She can't get the picture of her grandmother out of her head. James brushes close to her, and then walks down the ramp. He calls back at her to start singing. The talking stops and everyone looks up at Rosa.

Rosa holds the mike so tightly that it's hurting her hand. She feels tight inside also. Rosa tries to listen for the music. But her own heartbeat is far too loud.

"Sing!" James calls up to her. "Sing, kid, or you're out in the cold."

The band stops. Rosa feels her face go hot.

"OK," she hears James say loudly. "Go for it once more, then that's it. I don't have the time for this kind of game playing around my place. I got to think of . . ."

The music cuts James off. But still Rosa cannot sing. The events of her life swim all around her. With May soon dead, what will living in New York do for her? What does her stupid dream mean?

Rosa opens her mouth to sing. But all that comes out is a shaky uptight sound. She feels like she's going to scream any minute. She can't get the music out! It's pushing at her throat. Why can't it get out? Stop! Stop! She thinks, someone stop the music before it burns a hole through my head! Stop! My head is splitting open.

"Hold it!" James comes toward Rosa as the band stops playing. He takes the mike out of

Rosa's hand.

"I can't do it!" Rosa hears herself cry.

"No kidding!" James is steaming mad. "You can forget it, kid. Now that you have used up so much time for nothing. Next!" James calls out. But before Rosa steps down, he gets close to her. Under his breath, he says, "Forget singing, Big Eyes. But you can meet me tonight after the show."

Rosa is just about to hit James across the face when Ad steps up. Ad didn't hear what James said to her.

"Why aren't you singing?" Ad asks Rosa. "James put himself out to set up this tryout for you."

"I can't," Rosa says as she closes her eyes to the other faces in the room. "I need some air, Ad."

Ad doesn't move. He makes a sound with his foot. "You can have air after you sing. Or if you aren't going to sing, you can get the first train back to Burns. You're my responsibility since you ran away. You're in New York to sing. So sing now or else . . ."

Rosa doesn't stay around to hear any more of this. Before anyone can stop her, she's out the door of Street Scene and gone. She doesn't even catch the bus back. She just runs through the streets of the city, pushing past people. Her tears leave big wet circles on her dress.

Children are playing ball on the sidewalk and in the street. People are walking arm in arm. The sun shines. It's a great time for everyone . . . but Rosa. For her it's one of the worst days of her life.

She can't even remember where she's been running, but at last she sees Ad's apartment house ahead. Mike is sitting on the steps. Rosa tries to get in the side door, but Mike catches sight of her.

"Rosa!" he calls, tripping down the steps. "I've been waiting for you to come back from Street Scene. How was the tryout? Is James putting your name up in lights?"

By now Mike is standing still, looking at Rosa's face. "Trouble, baby?" he asks.

"Oh, no!" Rosa laughs loudly through her tears. "I can't sing. I had to stand in Street Scene and be put down by that stupid James. My brother is making me go back to Burns because I let him down. But really, life couldn't be better."

Rosa's laugh turns back to tears. She puts her hands over her face and sinks down on the steps. Mike is close beside Rosa, but at this moment it doesn't feel right to say anything.

Mike is close beside Rosa, but it doesn't feel
right to say anything.

For a long while they sit together on the warm steps.

When Rosa is ready to talk, she tells Mike what happened at Street Scene. Mike listens with his head thrown back. When Rosa is done, he spits on the sidewalk. "James needs a good pounding. Maybe Luther and me will take a walk over there tonight and . . ."

"Cool off, Mike." Rosa feels her eyes burn. "It was more than that. I wasn't able to sing at all. James turns me off all right, but it was my grandmother I couldn't stop thinking about. Now I'll never sing again . . ."

Mike kicks his legs out. "You will, baby, you will. Then you got to learn to keep guys like James in their place. As for Ad," Mike's face splits into a big smile, "I've never seen him dig any other girl like he does his sister. He's just mad about something. Maybe he got gas eating at Street Scene. The food there is the worst! And another thing, baby . . ."

"You sound like you're practicing your teacher trip," Rosa says, giving Mike a push.

Mike puts on his t-shirt. "I better look the part then. Besides, the sun is going down."

Rosa stands up. "Mike, what were you going to say?"

"Just this, baby. One of these days Ad may just have to give you up. Then any other guy who wants you will have to fight me!"

"Mike!" Rosa says into his face. "Any men who have to fight around me had better find a different girl to do it over. Understand?"

"Here comes Ad," Mike says, happy that he will not have to answer that one. Rosa turns and sees Ad coming up the street. He's moving fast. Coming closer, he sees Rosa.

"Rosa, where were you?" he calls to her. "I was really shaken up!" He runs up the steps two at a time. Then he sees Rosa's face and stops dead. Tears are streaming from her eyes. Ad takes her face in his hands. He can hardly get the words out. "Oh, Rosa, I really gave you a hard time, didn't I? That was blind of me not to dig what was happening there with James. Come on, little sister, enough rain for today. Right, Mike? If you sing, you sing. If you don't, you don't. As for going back to Burns, forget I ever said it. You stay with me. After high school is over, I'll help you get another kind of job. That way you can stay with me in New York for good."

Rosa puts her arms around Ad. "I love you, Ad," she says.

Ad looks away from Mike, but Mike will not let this moment pass by him for the world. He feels stupid, and so he has to say something.

"Ad," he says, making his words sound high. "I love you. Will you be mine forever? Oh, say you will."

"You just know how good I got it, man," Ad says, looking down at Mike over his glasses. "You wish Rosa were *your* sister."

"No, not my sister," Mike laughs, jumping down to the sidewalk facing up at Ad. "But she's going to be my girl, so help me."

"Work hard, live clean, and I might let you have her," Ad laughs.

Rosa pushes Ad down to where Mike is. "Will you two cool it. Let's go eat."

"All right!" says Ad. "Come on, Mike. Let's all hit the Mexican restaurant on 137th Street."

Rosa walks up the sidewalk with Ad and Mike. She knows she'll have many things to think about when she's by herself . . . her grandmother, her music, what Mike means to her. But right now she just feels like kicking back and putting her troubles aside. They'll still be waiting around for me when I get up tomorrow morning, she thinks.

9

Stopping the Fight

"Come on, Rosa," says Jill, opening the apartment door. "I know we can stop Luther and Mike if we're fast enough!"

It's evening and Jill and Rosa are listening to Ad's tapes. It's been two days since Rosa's tryout at Street Scene. No one, not even Ad, has talked to Rosa about it. They all want to give her space to think about what she's going to do.

Luther told Jill that tonight after dark there's going to be a showdown. He and Mike will be fighting some guys who turned Willy in to the cops for dope. Jill wants Rosa to go with her to the place where the fight will be. It's going to be in a walkway in back of an old workshop that Mike and Luther know about.

Rosa thinks Jill's idea is really off-the-wall. She tries to reason with her. "Ad told me to stay out of this, Jill," Rosa says. "Besides, I can't stop Mike. He knows I don't dig his fighting, but he does what he wants anyway. And one more thing. It's dangerous for us to go over to that part of the city by ourselves."

"Rosa," Jill says tightly, "Mike likes you more than any girl he's met. Luther told me. I know you can help. He'll listen to you."

Rosa brushes back her hair. She knows she had better give in . . . Jill isn't about to let up until she does. Besides, if there's any way she could keep Mike from fighting . . .

"OK," Rosa says, as she closes the window. "I think it's a stupid idea, but I'll go with you."

Jill throws an arm around Rosa. "Maybe we can get to the workshop before those street guys show. Then we can get Luther and Mike to leave with us."

"I'll bet you're the kind of kid that used to wish on a star," Rosa says.

Jill looks at Rosa for a moment. "Yes, I did," she says. "Didn't you?"

"Not much," Rosa throws out, thinking that she must be really out-of-it to go with Jill. "Let's get this over with."

Rosa and Jill leave the apartment and head toward 140th Street West. The sky is getting dark when they reach the workshop. There isn't a soul in sight. But a big green car is across the walkway with its headlights on bright.

"The car is bad news," Jill says to Rosa under her breath. "The boys use a car to light up where the fight will be. Guess they want to see who they're hitting! Most of the time they rip off the car, but they got this one from James White."

"They're like animals," Rosa says in a cold way, thinking she could have done without hearing James' name today. "I think we should let them all attack each other. If I get caught here, Jill, my name will be mud with Ad."

Jill is not listening to Rosa. She's looking up at an open window of the workshop. "What do you want to bet Luther and Mike are in there? I'll bet they're using the workshop for a lookout. They must have tripped the window lock. But how did they get up there? Oh, look, Rosa, under the window. We can use those boxes and boards to climb up. Let's go."

Rosa is starting to wish she had listened to Ad. As they get close, Rosa and Jill don't say a word. Jill shows with her hands that she wants Rosa to help her. They put the boxes and boards on a big can sitting under the open window. Then Rosa helps her climb up. When Jill is up, she gives Rosa a handhold. In a few seconds, both the girls are through the window and into the workshop. It's so dark that Rosa can't see a thing. The only sound she hears is her heartbeat. Rosa thinks to herself, I want to go back. If we're found in here, they'll book us for robbery. What a big help that would be for Mike!

"Hold it where you are!"

Rosa and Jill scream and fall back against the wall. Rosa feels hands on her. She can't scream again because someone is holding a hand over her mouth. She can't breath. She fights to push the hand away. All of a sudden she hears a boy say, "It's Rosa!"

At last she's free to move. As her eyes get used to the dark, she makes out Luther and Mike standing in the room.

"What do you two think you're doing following us here?" Mike sounds ready to hit someone. "Whatever your game is, you can get right back out the way you came in . . . now!"

"We didn't follow you," Jill says shaking.

Mike turns to Luther. "Then how did they know where to come to?"

Jill steps up to Mike. "Luther told us and I'm not going to leave without him."

"Luther, baby," Mike says with a mean laugh. "Time to go home now. Your mother is here for you."

"Stop it, Mike!" Jill cries. "I don't want Luther to get killed."

"What you want is not important to me, Jill," Mike fires back. "But you better listen good to what I want. You and Luther can be love birds some other time. But I want Rosa out of here now. Do you hear what I'm saying to you, Jill?"

"Mike—" Rosa comes close to him.

"No more words!" Mike hammers the wall with his hand.

Rosa goes to the window. "Forget it, Jill. Let's get out of here. I told you it was no use." She looks back at Mike. "I'll go, Mike. But I want you to know that I think this is really stupid. There's nothing strong about fighting. You can't help Willy at all this way. He will not have a friend in the world if you're killed or in a cage. And what about your teaching dream? Dead people aren't so hot at getting through school!"

"Get out!" Mike screams.

"OK," Rosa says as she climbs out the window. "But one more thing. Anything that was going on with you and me . . . forget it. It's over." Rosa gets down off the boxes. Jill comes next.

"What about you?" Mike asks Luther.

All of a sudden Rosa hears a far away sound that she knows well by now. Luther has heard it, too.

"It's the law, Mike!" Luther backs down from the window. "Those hot characters that want to nail Willy must be running scared. They went to the cops. Let's beat it!"

"Get the lights off in that car," Mike cries to Luther. He jumps from the window and lands on his feet. He pushes Rosa toward the walkway.

"Get out of here!"

"No, Mike," cries Jill. "You and Luther go in the car. Rosa and I will stay here and wait for the cops. We'll keep them talking while you get away."

"She's right, Mike," Luther calls, turning the wheels of the car. "They aren't going to hurt the girls. Come on."

Mike doesn't move.

"Mike!" Rosa hears the cop cars getting louder. "Go! Get out of here! I don't want you taken in. Will you listen to me for once? Get away from here!"

Mike looks hard at Rosa. It seems to her that years pass in that one minute. At last Mike starts to move toward the car. Rosa sees how tightly he's holding himself as he climbs in. Luther turns the key. The car starts to back out across the walkway.

"If you get hurt, Rosa . . ." Mike calls.

"I'll be OK," she waves her hand. "Go!"

The green car drives away from Rosa and Jill. They stand together on the sidewalk. Rosa passes her hand across her eyes. Her head hurts. Soon after the boys leave, three cop cars pull up. Rosa and Jill stand waiting. They say nothing. A cop gets out of the first car and comes up to them.

"What are you two doing on the street after dark?" he asks.

Jill smiles. "Oh, just taking in the night."

"Too hot to stay inside," Rosa says. She can feel her heart race. She can't believe that she is able to talk to the cops at all. She thinks she must be getting used to New York.

"Now, girls," says the cop. He smiles, but his eyes are hard. "I get real touchy when I don't get what I want. You wouldn't be waiting to meet Mike Match and Luther Marks here would you? We got the word that they are looking for some trouble tonight."

"What kind of trouble?" Rosa asks, opening her eyes big.

"Fighting trouble."

"Well," Jill is moving up the sidewalk, "we aren't needed here, then. I wouldn't be caught dead anywhere close to street fighting. Would you, Rosa? And you know those boys aren't doing any fighting with us around. We wouldn't hear of it!"

The cop looks at Jill and Rosa. "I don't know what you two are up to, but you better get home fast. If I see you on the street in 15 minutes, I'm running you both in. I don't want no trouble on my beat, understand? You would do well to remember what I say. And you can tell your boyfriends when you see them."

Rosa and Jill say nothing.

"If I catch those boys of yours fighting," the cop goes on, "I'll see that the judge throws the book at them." Rosa starts to move away, but the cop puts his foot out. "Aren't you Ad's sister? I seen you with Match and Marks the other night. Does your brother know where you are?"

Rosa looks right through the cop. "Yes," she says turning away. "I am Ad's sister. But I'm a big girl now and I do what I want."

"Not big enough," the cop says hotly. He climbs in his car and waves to the other cops. The cars move off down the street. Rosa and Jill stand still for a few seconds. And then, without a word, they start to run. They don't stop until they are on Jill's street. They fall down on the apartment house steps, out of breath.

"What a warm guy that cop is," laughs Rosa.

"He's OK." Jill pushes her hair out of her face. "He's got a hard beat. You can't believe some of the other cops around here. They make this guy look great!"

Jill and Rosa sit thinking about all that happened. Now that the hard part is over, they both feel scared. They don't say much. Rosa just feels good that the fight didn't come off. After a while, Rosa says good-by to Jill. She heads down the street toward Ad's place. Walking, she pictures Mike in the green car. But then she throws back her head and looks up at Ad's apartment. The light is on in his rooms. She remembers that it was daylight when she left. Ad had gone to work. There were no lights on! With a start she thinks, who's up there in Ad's place?

Feeling herself start to shake for the first time that night, Rosa goes up the steps to the door . . .

10

Willy Turns Up

Rosa lets herself into Ad's apartment and finds her brother waiting for her!

"Ad," she cries. "What are you doing here? Aren't you working?"

"I had to get off work," Ad says, moving away from the window. "There was trouble at home."

"What do you mean?" Rosa's heart sinks at his words. "What kind of trouble?"

"I got a phone call from the cops," Ad tells her. She sees his face tighten. His hands are shaking. "They said I needed to get home and find my sister. What's this all about, Rosa? I told you to keep out of that thing with Mike and Luther. Why didn't you do what I said?"

Rosa can see that Ad has had a scare. She knows what she means to him. She feels very bad. He's tried to do so much for her. Still, she wants him to understand.

"Jill thought we could stop the fight," she says.

"Well, I guess you did that OK," Ad tells her. He's happy to see Rosa, but he still feels uptight after all that's happened. "But you could have been hurt badly. Those guys are real mean when they're fighting. When they're like that, they don't think of no one but themselves."

Rosa eyes Ad evenly. "Why did you say we stopped the fight? How did you know that?"

Ad walks back to the window and looks out at the night. "Mike came by looking for you. He told me everything." Rosa sees Ad reach over and turn the light on and off.

"What are you doing?" she asks.

"Mike's down the street," Ad tells her. He does the light again. "He's waiting for you to get home. I told him I would let him know you're OK this way."

Rosa walks over to stand by Ad. "Why didn't he just wait for me?"

"I'm not sure. Sounded like it was something you said to him." Ad looks right at Rosa and takes hold of her. "You're getting used to New York, little sister. But let's not have any more of this with the cops. You got to stay friendly with these guys. You never know when you'll have a need for them. And you had better keep an eye on Mike, too. He's getting a little too hot for my sister, if you ask me."

Rosa turns away from Ad. She doesn't want to think about Mike right now. There's something else they have to talk about first.

"Ad," says Rosa, feeling tears come into her eyes. "There's something you should know."

Ad sits down in a chair and takes off his glasses. "Don't say it that way, Rosa. If it's bad news, I've had enough for one night!"

Rosa gets out Mr. Moe's letter and hands it to Ad. "It's about May."

Putting his glasses back on, Ad reads the letter once. He studies Rosa's face, and then reads it again.

"Great old May," Ad says at last. He's quiet for a moment looking out the window. "I guess I thought she would live forever, but no one does. I'm sure going to miss her. We couldn't have made it without her. Right, Rosa?" Then before Rosa can answer, Ad shakes his head. "Good thing she's got her own money to live on. I don't have enough in my savings for that. But I can sure help her out if she has need." Ad looks at Rosa's face. "You know, little sister, we don't want to think of May being gone, but we still got our own lives to live. We can help her out as much as we can without giving up ourselves. You hear me, Rosa?"

Rosa plays with a string coming out of the chair arm. "I don't know," she says slowly.

Ad puts the letter aside. "When did you get this?" he asks.

"Just before I went to sing," Rosa says, trying not to remember how she felt at the club.

"I get it now." Ad stands up and walks around the room. "It wasn't only that you don't dig James. It was thinking about May that tripped you up at the tryout. Why didn't you tell me? Couldn't you trust me enough?"

Ad's words burn through Rosa. She says, "It isn't trust, Ad." All of a sudden Rosa thinks back on all the years. "You know we only had ourselves when we were little. Ad and Rosa against the rest of the world, remember? I always knew I had you. But here in New York I have to do it on my own. It's my singing—not yours. It's true. The letter about May was throwing me off that night. But I did not want help from anyone, even you. What happened was, I couldn't get May out of my head. I just wasn't able to sing." Rosa looks away from Ad. "When the words wouldn't come out, I knew it was because I should be home with grand-mother . . . So that's what I'm going to do. I'm going back to Burns and give up singing."

"Rosa," Ad says with a troubled look. "Remember what I just told you? You said you want to live your own life. Giving up your music and going back to May for good is living May's life. You can't do that. Look, James will let you sing again if I ask him. I did something for him once, and he can pay me back this way. Go back to Burns for your last school year. Come to New York next summer. By then I know you'll be ready." Ad walks around fast, feeling somehow that he isn't getting through to Rosa. "Look, I got to get back to work. I'm sorry to cut out like this. You think on what I said, OK? Eat something."

Rosa puts her hand on Ad's arm. "I'll think on it," she says slowly. "I promise." Ad goes out the door. Rosa locks it and then listens to Ad's steps on the stairs. After a few minutes she feels the hot night around her. She thinks it might be better outside, and so she goes down to the street.

Sitting on the steps Rosa is happy not to be with anyone. There are so many thoughts moving inside her again . . . May, Mike and his fighting, Willy and his troubles, her own singing. Music has been part of Rosa ever since she can remember. Without my singing, Rosa thinks, I might as well die. How can I give up so soon? Ad's right about that. I need to sing the way other people need to breathe air.

Rosa puts her arms around her legs. She keeps thinking about Mike and Willy and singing. Everyone needs some way to keep it together, she says to herself. Some ways are better than others. Willy has dope, Mike has fighting, and I have . . . had singing.

After a long time, Rosa sees someone coming up the sidewalk. She looks hard and as he gets halfway up the street, Rosa knows it's Mike.

"Hi, Rosa!" he calls. "Want to go for a walk?" Rosa looks at Mike. When he sees how quiet she is, he asks, "Are we really on the outs, baby? I know you can't stand the fighting. But give me time to work it out in my own way. Will you walk with me?"

"OK, Mike," Rosa says. "I'll go."

They walk down the street together. There are many people out, but Mike comes close to Rosa and talks under his breath.

"Willy's around," he says evenly. "A friend saw him and said he's looking for me."

Rosa looks at Mike to see how he's feeling about this. "Are you going to try and help him?"

"If I can . . . and if he finds me."

Rosa and Mike walk on. They go by apartment houses and through streets Rosa has never seen. They come to a part of New York with many run-down houses. It doesn't look to Rosa like anyone lives in them. She doesn't see any people around at all. There are few street lights, and it's hard to see in the dark. On one side of the street, there's a playground. On the other side is a dark apartment house with a small yard. It's very quiet. Mike stops. Rosa feels her hair stand on end . . . someone else is around here! She can feel it.

"Look at this place," Mike says, making Rosa jump. "Not a soul here now, but Willy and I lived here as little kids. That's how we met. I wanted to come by tonight for some reason."

Rosa eyes the apartment. There's a catwalk across some windows. Someone must have started to work on the place and then left it. All of a sudden, Rosa cries out.

"Mike, look! Someone's up there on the catwalk."

Rosa feels Mike start. As they both look, they hear an outrageously mad sound . . . like an animal laughing. Mike moves closer to the apartment, still looking up.

"Willy!" Mike calls out. "That's you, isn't it?"

"How you know I was here, brother?" someone blasts down from the catwalk.

Rosa thinks, that's Willy all right!

"I didn't know," Mike tells him. "Man, get off that catwalk and come down here so we can talk!"

"Who you got with you?" Willy wants to

97

Willy makes an outrageously mad sound . . .
like an animal laughing.

know. It sounds to Rosa as if Willy's eating rocks.

"Not the cops, brother," says Mike.

For a minute there's no sound. Then, "You got that girl with you, Mike? Is that how it is now? You think I'll talk around her? I'm not that stupid, man."

"Willy!" Mike calls loudly. "How did I know you would be here? It don't make no difference about Rosa. She's a friend, too. The cops are all over this town trying to find you, boy. I heard you were looking for me, but how was I going to find you?"

Rosa comes close to Mike. "I'll walk home," she says so Willy doesn't hear.

"You stay put, baby!" Mike fires at her.

"Wasn't me done that killing," Willy calls to Mike. "But now that they got me on dope, they'll try to run me in for this, too."

"You're wrong, Willy." Mike hears the catwalk moving. "They know it isn't your finger-prints on the gun. They just want to trip you out, man. You got to give yourself up and clear your name. If you stay away it looks like you really did do that guy in."

Rosa hears Willy laugh. She's standing so close to Mike that she feels him get tight when he hears the laugh. "He's on the needle again," Mike says. He throws back his head and calls loudly, "Willy, get off that catwalk. I can't talk to you so good when you're up there. I can't even see you!"

Willy says something that Mike can't hear. "What?" Mike calls. "I didn't catch it, Willy."

"I'm broke," Willy says again. "I got nothing and I need it bad, Mike."

"OK," Mike looks at Rosa to see if she knows what's happening. "We'll talk about it, but you got to come down here first."

"I'm not coming down until you're alone," Willy says.

For a long while Mike says nothing. Rosa knows he's thinking about what to do next. At last he turns to her. "We're going, baby. I don't want you out in this part of the city by yourself. I'll come back for Willy."

"Mike . . . ," Rosa starts to say something and then stops herself. Mike can't be talked to when he knows what he wants. They move off. Mike looks up at the catwalk. "Stay there, Willy. Don't move. I'll run Rosa home and be right back. Hear me, Willy?"

Willy laughs again. Rosa and Mike can hear the catwalk move against the apartment. They go off down the street at a run.

At last they reach Ad's street. Mike turns Rosa around so she's facing him. "Do you know what he wants to use the money for?"

"Food?" Rosa asks, trying to catch her breath.

"Don't bank on it," Mike laughs. "More like dope."

"Are you going to give it to him?" Rosa's eyes are big.

"I don't know . . ." Mike is asking himself the same question.

"Leave me here, Mike," Rosa says.

"OK," Mike turns to go back.

"What if Willy isn't there?" Rosa calls after him.

"It's his life, beautiful," Mike says into the night. "He's got to do for himself someday."

Just like I do, Rosa thinks. She turns around to see Mike a last time, but now there is only dark where he was a minute before.

11

A Cold Wind

The next morning Jill tells Rosa she's just seen Mike. By the time he got back to the old apartment house, Willy was gone. It's a very hot day in the city. All Rosa and Jill want to do is sit peacefully on the steps. Warm days, living with her brother, having Mike and her other new friends . . . . Rosa thinks to herself, is New York getting into my blood? Would I miss Burns if I never saw it again? And what about my singing? Will something ever come of it? If not, would I be happy working in a factory or someplace else?

"What's happening?" Rosa's thoughts are broken by Luther. He walks over and drops down beside Jill.

Jill runs her hand across her face. "What does it look like? Not much can happen when it's this hot!"

"That's what you think, Shyness and Light," Luther tries to kiss Jill. "A lot goes on when it's hot!"

"Cut it out!" Jill cries, pushing Luther off the steps.

Mike has come up, too. He sits by Rosa. "You hear about Willy?" he asks her.

"Yes, Jill told me." Rosa's face is close to Mike's. "You know, Mike, if I had walked home by myself last night . . ."

"And gotten killed? Hot idea, baby. I don't want to talk about it. Willy has to stay clean and get it together in his own life. If he doesn't, what can I do for him?"

"Southern?" Luther says to Rosa, trying to get them off Willy. "What would you say about going to high school here in the city with Jill and me? We can all kick back and have a cool time our last year. We have a winning basketball team. Right, Jill?"

"If you say so, Luther," Jill is still mad about Luther trying to kiss her while her friends were looking.

Luther turns to Mike. "You should have stayed in school. You would have been the star on the team."

"Thanks, man!" Mike kicks at the steps. "I told you before not to talk about the school thing. Don't you ever listen?"

"Come on." Luther gets Jill up. "It's too tight around here for me. Let's go get cold drinks to cool this character off."

"Great," Mike throws out. "Get lost!"

After Jill and Luther go, Rosa and Mike sit together on the steps. Rosa thinks about how Mike must feel with all his friends in school. It makes her sad. There are a lot of things she doesn't like about school. Still, she knows how important it is. Mike doesn't say much about how he feels. But she knows he's like her. That means there's a lot of hurt he keeps inside.

As if he could read her thoughts, Mike says, "School isn't for me right now. I can't take all the stupid rules. Teachers think they're so important. One day last year I just had enough. I took my coat and basketball and cut out. And that was it, man. I never went back no more. I like the job I got at the gas station better than being in school."

Rosa knows just how that is . . . being made to do things you don't want to do. She pictures her grandmother and a tight feeling comes over her. But then she feels badly. May will not be around to tell her what to do much longer.

"I'm never going to run for President," Mike goes on, "but I would like to help kids like Willy get out from under. That's one reason I want to teach. I know it means some day I got to get more schooling. But I'm going to be the judge of when I do that. No one tells Mike Match what to do!"

Rosa thinks of all the things Ad and Mike have said to her in the last week. They have gotten her to think about living for herself and being her own boss.

Sometimes Rosa is shy around Mike—he can be so explosive. But now she wants to touch him. She puts her hand on his arm. He starts and looks down at her. Then he takes her hand in his. They sit this way, seeing nothing but each other until Luther and Jill come back. When he sees his friends, Mike drops Rosa's hand. But he keeps smiling at her with his eyes. Luther and Jill come up the steps and hand around sodas. When he gets to Rosa, Luther holds her drink above her head.

"Southern," Luther closes his eyes. He moves lightly on the steps like he's floating on air. "Help us cool off. Make us a windy day."

"How?" Rosa can't help laughing at Luther.

"Sing the blues for us," he says.

Mike gives Luther the bad eye and starts to stand up. Rosa puts a hand out toward Mike. He stops, trying to tell what she's thinking.

"It's OK," she says to him. No one moves. It's as if Rosa holds them with her thoughts. Then the music starts to well up inside of her like it used to do at home. She looks at Mike, Jill and Luther. There is no talking at all. And at last, Rosa starts to sing the blues.

"Baby, I been missing you, all my hardships coming through, think I'm going to love you all my days . . ."

As Rosa sings, other kids on the street walk over to listen, too. One boy brings out a guitar and plays along with Rosa. The sounds float into the hot air. Rosa closes her eyes and sings. She moves with her song as the music finds its way into her soul. She forgets there is anything in the world but her song. Now the people around her are all rocking too. Like Rosa, they have closed their eyes. No one sees Ad, who is just returning from work. He sits down beside Rosa on the steps. At last Rosa stops. When she does, it feels as if the hot air blasts back to take over where the music just was.

Rosa shakes her head. She catches Ad's eye, and they give each other a secret smile. People are calling out, "Sing it! Sing it, baby!" Rosa waves her hand to say, "No more!" In a flash Ad stands up on the steps. He raises his hands over his head so people will listen to him.

"If you want to hear Rosa sing," Ad says loudly from the steps, "James wants her to try out for the summer show over at his club, Street Scene."

"Do it, Rosa," Harriet tells her.

"You'll be great this time," Jill puts in. She gives Luther a kick in the leg.

"Right!" he says. "Maybe James will let us come root for you at the tryout, Southern."

Rosa looks at Mike, waiting for him to say something. Mike doesn't move. From the look on his face, it's clear to Rosa where he stands. He's happy she can have another try at Street Scene, but she knows he will not say that. He thinks she should do what she wants, not what the others want her to do. Now it's the music Rosa hears talking to her. And she knows she must listen. There is no turning away from the music inside her.

"OK," Rosa says at last. "I'll give it another go!"

Rosa's friends jump up and down laughing and pushing each other. Ad has no words for showing how he feels. Mike takes a long drink, and then he says, "That's the way to play the game, baby."

By this time even more people are on the sidewalk. They are trying to find out what's happening. A boy Luther knows from school calls out, "What is this, a party?"

Ad's eyes flash. This gives him a great idea. "It sure is," he says. "I'm throwing a party right now for my little sister. Everyone up to my place."

"Far out!" someone cries. The people on the sidewalk move like a wave toward the apartment house door.

Ad takes out some bills and hands the money to Mike and Luther. "Go get some chips and drinks," he tells them. "And as much ice as you can bring back."

"How about music?" Luther waves at Rosa. "Are you the music machine, Southern?"

"Right, Luther." Rosa's head is so light she feels like she just climbed a mountain.

"Rosa," Ad calls. He is going up the steps two at a time. "I hear tell there's a party somewhere around here."

Rosa goes up after him. "Right, Ad. Let's crash it!" Ad and Rosa go in, leaving Mike and Luther on the sidewalk. As Mike and Luther take off to get food, Mike hears someone call his name. He stops. Coming toward him are two boys that were in the halfway house with Willy. Mike feels himself get hot. With these two, trouble is never far away.

"What's up, Thomas?" Mike wants to know.

"It's about Willy," the boy named Thomas says, coming up. He looks around slowly.

"There are no cops here. You can talk." Mike takes a breath trying to stay cool.

"Willy told us to find you."

"So, and what did he say?"

108

Thomas gives Luther a hard look. "Who's this guy?" he asks.

"A friend," Mike says, feeling tighter every second. "You can trust him to keep quiet. Now go on."

Thomas moves his feet around and looks down. The other boy doesn't say a word. "He needs money real bad. He's out of pony," Thomas says. Mike starts at the sound of this word. These characters have a new word for dope every week, he thinks.

Mike moves away from Thomas. "You can tell Willy he's getting nothing from me for dope," Mike says. "Not now or ever. There's no more to say on that."

"He says you're the only friend he's got," Thomas goes on like he hasn't heard Mike. "Willy's going to do a job in a house on the East Side." Thomas comes close to Mike and looks around again. Mike sees that he's shaking all over. Thomas says, "He knows a housekeeper who can get us into this pad. These people got everything, Willy says. They're out of town for two weeks. We'll clean up. He wants you in on it. And your friend, I guess, if you say so. How about it, Mike? Willy wants you to meet us at the graveyard on West 155th Street tonight. We're going to work it all out then."

Without thinking, Mike steps back as if to get

away from Thomas. He sees that Luther's eyes are big, but Luther says nothing. Mike thinks to himself, I can't believe these guys. Are they out of their heads? Robbery! And Willy—he must be really tripped out.

Thomas gives Mike a questioning look. Mike and Luther have kept their eyes on Thomas. But now they look at each other. In a second, they communicate what they're thinking. Slowly, Luther moves around in back of the two boys.

"Well," Thomas asks Mike, "can we count you in, or don't you got the guts to do the job?"

In a flash, Mike takes hold of Thomas and throws him to the sidewalk. Luther pushes the other boy to the steps and pulls back his arms. There's blood on the side of Thomas' face as he looks up at Mike. What Thomas sees scares him to death. Mike's eyes are as cold as ice. He looks right at Thomas for a long, long time. Thomas thinks he can't stand it another second. Then under his breath, Mike starts to talk. He says each word slowly so Thomas misses nothing.

"Listen to me good so you can go back and tell Willy everything I said." Mike takes a breath and lets it out again. "Willy boy is like a brother to me, you hear? And it's guys like you that got him on dope. It's you that got him into all this trouble. Now you're going to help me get him out of it. You tell him to forget that little event with the housekeeper. If he knows what's good for him, he will. If he don't, he's going to have me to answer to. You tell him to stay out of this and to find me by tomorrow night. He knows where—but not in no graveyard, you understand?" Mike raises Thomas up by the shirt. "Understand me?"

"Yes!" Thomas screams. "Let go, man."

"You're going to feel it a lot more," Mike says through his teeth, "if Willy does this job. You got a good memory?"

"Yes!" Thomas screams again.

"Great," Mike says. "Because if Willy gets hurt, you're going to wish you were dead." He gets up off Thomas. When Thomas stands up again, Mike takes him and throws him up the sidewalk. Luther does the same thing with the other boy.

"Now get out of here real quick," Mike calls. He's steaming mad and he feels like pounding them both into the sidewalk. Mike and Luther look at each other. Luther sees there are tears in Mike's eyes. "This is real bad, Luther," Mike says, turning his face away. He doesn't want Luther to see that he's crying.

"Come on, Mike," Luther tells him. "Let's go get food for the party. There's not much you can do now."

Mike and Luther go by the steps to Ad's apartment. Mike starts. Rosa is sitting on the first step. She doesn't move. "You heard?" Mike asks, as he brushes his hand across his eyes. Rosa shakes her head yes.

Mike tries to tell what she's thinking. Does she see that it could be all over for Willy? "Sometimes you got to fight," Mike says. Rosa says nothing for a long time. Mike doesn't move. At last she looks up at him.

"I'm trying to understand," she says. "But I still don't like it at all."

"I know," Mike tells her.

"There has to be a better way, doesn't there?" Rosa says.

"Maybe," Mike answers. But inside he feels that here in the streets, fighting is the only way there is. "We'll be back soon."

Mike and Luther move off down the sidewalk. Rosa stands up and looks at them go. To Rosa, the robbery talk is like a cold danger- ous wind. Even if the air is hot, the cold wind still cuts into their world.

12

Rosa Tries Again

The weekend comes at last. Rosa is as ready as she ever will be to sing at Street Scene. James scares Rosa. And she feels like throwing up when he comes around her. But she has to sing at his club. She will just have to keep him in line. Once she gets her start, she can move on to another club. James is paying Ad back for a bet he lost. That's the only reason Rosa gets to sing again, and she knows it.

This time Rosa's friends will be at Street Scene for her tryout. James doesn't like anyone under 18 in his club. But he says it's OK this once because the place is closed in the daytime.

Rosa is in Ad's apartment walking up and down the living room. She tried reading a book but couldn't keep her eyes on the page. As soon as Ad gets back from having his hair cut, they'll go to Street Scene. Someone pounds on the door. Rosa answers it and in walks Mike.

"Hi!" he says, coming into the room.

Rosa is too scared about the tryout to find words to say. She looks at Mike. Something about him is different today. He's standing with his head down, moving his feet around.

"What's wrong with you?" Rosa asks.

Mike says nothing. But he holds out his hand and gives Rosa a small box. Shyly, Rosa opens it. Inside the box is a circle pin with pink and blue lines running through it. Rosa can hardly hear Mike, but he says, "Hold it up to the sunlight." She walks to the window and lets light play on the pin. The pink and blue run together beautifully. She looks up at Mike.

"It was my grandmother's," he tells Rosa. "When I was a kid, I lived with her for a time just like you do. She left me this pin when she died. I want you to have it for the tryout, and then you can keep it."

Rosa touches the pin, looking at the way the sun makes it shine. Then she says, "I can't take this, Mike. Your grandmother wanted you to have it."

"Well, baby," Mike starts out. He sounds like the same old Mike again, but Rosa catches a smile around his eyes. "If you don't want it, I'm going to see what I can get for it at the races."

"Cut it out, Mike," Rosa says. She's happy that he's playing around again. "If that's how it is, you can come over here and pin it on my dress for me."

Mike is putting the pin on Rosa when they hear Ad in the hall talking.

"I better split," Mike says as he backs toward the door. "You look . . . well, what can I say?" Rosa stands by the window without moving. All of a sudden Mike walks back to her. He takes her face in his hands and kisses her for a long time.

At last she pushes him back, laughing. "Mike!" Rosa cries. "You aren't leaving me enough breath to sing with."

Mike moves out the door just as Ad comes in. "Sing hot, baby," he says, and then he's gone.

Ad looks at Rosa for a long moment. He sees that her eyes are shiny. "Ready?" he asks.

"Ready!" Rosa says. They go out the door after Mike.

In an hour Rosa and Ad reach Street Scene. Mike has just come in, too. He sits down with Luther, Jill and Harriet. Rosa sees James right away. She holds tightly to Ad's arm. The club looks very much the same as before. There are a lot of people sitting around in the dark holding drinks. James is working on the lights. When he's through, he walks to the back of the room where Rosa is.

There is nothing friendly about his face. He

and Ad shake hands, and then he turns to Rosa. She doesn't know how she can ever let go of Ad to sing. But James answers her question. "I don't like giving you another go, Big Eyes," he says. "I'll tell you that right off the bat. But I got no say about it. Big Ad here was holding something over my head. Anyhow, this is it. So get up there and give me the golden sounds they tell me you got."

James turns his back on Rosa and walks off. For another minute Rosa just stands with Ad. She remembers when they were kids. The first time they were going to live in Burns, they waited hand in hand like this for the train. Ad always looked as if nothing could scare him. Even if this wasn't true, it helped Rosa. Now Ad comes close to her. He says under his breath, "I'm with you, Rosa, whatever happens."

Now is the time, Rosa thinks. She lets go of Ad's hand and walks up the ramp. She feels all the eyes follow her as she comes into the bright light. James hands her the mike. He gives her a look that makes her feel like running away. You aren't going to scare me out of here, James, she thinks. But she stands very still. There is not a sound in the room and everyone is looking at her. All of a sudden James calls out, "Music! Play it!" And he jumps off the ramp.

The light is full on Rosa. It feels so hot that her face burns. She thinks she might fall any minute. Somewhere out in the dark are Ad, Mike and the others. Rosa puts her hand on the pin Mike gave her. It makes her feel strong.

"Sing!" she hears James scream. Just like last time, her timing is off. She will have to start over. The band stops. James comes up. He looks right at Rosa. His shiny, wet-looking hair, big teeth and tight face make Rosa think of a beaver.

"Get out of my place," James says through his teeth. "You're making me look bad before all these people. I want you gone!"

The more Rosa looks at James, the more he looks like a beaver. Without thinking what she's doing, Rosa laughs in his face.

"Get out!" James is steaming mad now.

Rosa knows she's not thinking clearly, but she can't help herself. She looks over at the band and screams, "Play, I tell you. Play!"

Slowly the band starts up again. Rosa holds the mike up to her face. James is standing so close to her that she can hear his breath come and go. Rosa takes in air. And then the music that is always in her, floats out into the room.

"Got me a woman away down South and her home in another city,

"But here in this old town of mine, I got no living soul but me . . ."

James has moved back off the ramp. He can't believe how Rosa sings. He's never heard anyone so clear and strong before!

Now Rosa forgets everything in the world but her song. The blues are all around her. The dark room feels light to Rosa. She sings, moves and shakes, holding the mike like a baby. She feels like she will never stop. She closes her eyes and throws her head back and sings. She has never sounded like this before. The other people in the room cannot move. She goes on and on. Even before the music stops, Rosa is sure she's done it. This time, she's going to make it. She's a hit!

At last Rosa does stop singing. She puts her head down over the mike and waits for the music to die out. No one in the room moves or says a word. Rosa loves this moment—all is quiet. The first sound she hears is James. He isn't at all friendly, but he says the words she most wants to hear.

"You just go yourself a job, kid. You can start singing here next week." James comes up to her. "What do you say?"

Rosa is feeling stronger every minute. She doesn't answer James right away. She just looks at him in a cold, hard way. Then she remembers a line from a TV show. "I'll sing at Street Scene, James," she says. "But you'll have to see my brother. He's my agent. We can talk money in the morning. Right now I'm going with my friends."

"I thought," James gives Rosa a secret smile, "maybe tonight, you and me . . ."

Rosa faces James. Now is the time to put him in his place. "What you thought is wrong," she says. "As I was saying before, I'm going out on the town. And not with you. If I work for you, there is one thing you better remember." Rosa looks at James to make sure he's listening. "I want you to keep your hands to yourself. Do you hear what I'm saying?"

Seeing James' face, Rosa has to keep back a smile. It's clear he doesn't like being talked to this way.

"Kid, if you couldn't sing . . ." he starts to say.

"Yes, but I can," Rosa cuts in. "Now, how about it, James?"

"OK." James holds out his hand. "You got your way, Big Eyes." Rosa and James shake hands.

Next thing she knows, Rosa's friends are all around her. Other people come up, too. Everyone tells her she's great . . . a real winner. Ad looks so happy, Rosa thinks to herself. That makes two of us.

Rosa pushes through the people and out of Street Scene. She wants to get some air. Ad stays behind to talk with James. Jill and Harriet come with Rosa. Now that she's outside, Rosa looks around for Mike.

"Mike's not here," Jill says. "He and Luther cut out as soon as you stopped singing."

So what if Mike took off, she thinks to herself. There's no reason why he should stay around. Rosa touches the pin on her dress. Still, she turns her head as if she thinks Mike will show up any second.

"Shake it off, Rosa," Harriet tells her. "Who knows where they went? Looking for trouble, I'll bet."

"Come on," says Jill. "I know where there's a party. You need a good time after singing that way. You can find another boy at the party."

"We'll go with you while you change." Harriet takes Rosa's arm.

"OK," Rosa says. "But let's wait for my brother." She can't think of any more to say. She knows she should be happy. Now she's going to sing in New York. After all, that's what was important. Still, something has changed. She can no longer keep Mike out of her head.

13

Scene in the Street

It's the day after Rosa's last tryout at Street Scene. Rosa is going to sing at the club for the summer. Ad has made sure James is going to pay her good money. For Rosa, life could not look better . . . if it weren't for Mike . . .

No one has seen Mike or Luther. But some friends told Ad there was a big robbery on the East Side last night. No one can learn anything because the cops aren't talking.

Rosa and Ad are sitting out on the steps eating donuts and drinking coffee. Rosa reads a letter from Sue. Her friend writes about how great their last school year is going to be.

"Oh, Ad," Rosa hits her brother in the side. "Sue says to give you a great big kiss. How about that?"

"That's cool," Ad says. Rosa sees a smile flash across Ad's face. He looks down at Rosa over the top of his glasses. "Guess I better take you back to Burns myself when the summer ends. I wouldn't want to hurt one of your friends for all the world, Rosa!"

"You're so full of it, Ad," Rosa says, pushing him.

Rosa sees Jill coming up the street. She knows right away that something has happened. Jill looks uptight and walks fast. Just as she is about to reach Ad's apartment house, a cop car comes slowly up the street. Rosa, Ad and Jill all turn and follow it with their eyes. In the back seat of the cop car are Mike and Luther. No one moves or says a word.

Rosa sees Mike say something to the cop driving the car. He pulls over. Very slowly, as if they hurt, Mike and Luther get out. Luther closes the car door and the cop drives off.

Rosa's heart sinks at the sight of Mike. It's as if life has been ripped right out of him. Like people in a play without words, Luther and Mike come up the steps. Their eyes are red. And they look like they haven't changed their clothes for a week. Now Rosa sees that Mike's shirt has blood all over it. Luther holds out his hand for Jill. They go off down the sidewalk with their heads close together. Once Jill turns around fast and looks back at Mike.

Mike stands at the foot of the steps with his head down. Rosa hears a sound come from him. For a minute she's not sure what he's doing. But then she sees Mike shaking and she knows he's crying. Rosa and Ad look at each other for a long moment. Then Ad takes Rosa's hand. He holds it tightly for a few seconds before he turns and goes inside.

After Ad leaves, Rosa walks down to Mike. Mike is still crying, but now he looks up at Rosa. Then he holds out his arms, and he and Rosa melt together. They sink down on the steps and just sit there. Mike is quiet so long that Rosa doesn't know if he'll ever talk again.

"Do you know?" he asks her at last. He holds her hand so tightly that it starts to hurt.

"I can guess," Rosa says. She looks at Mike. His eyes tell her what she doesn't want to believe.

"Willy's dead." Mike shakes as he says it.

"I'm so sorry, Mike," Rosa tells him. She touches his wet face with her fingers.

Mike sits back looking up the street. He feels Willy might come down the sidewalk with his one-sided run at any moment. "Yesterday he was here," Mike says slowly. "Today he's gone. No more Willy." Mike turns to Rosa. Tears run down his face. "Dope was Willy's downfall, Rosa," he tells her. "Willy felt like he just couldn't win the game of life at all."

Rosa waits for Mike to get it together. Then

she asks, "When did you find out about Willy, Mike?"

"Not until last night," Mike says. He closes his eyes. "A friend of mine got into Street Scene. He told Luther and me he knew where Willy was. You were just done singing, so we cut out. I wanted to wait for you. You were so great, but I just had to find Willy. Well," Mike stops, trying to find the words to go on, "we never did find him until it was too late. Someone had seen him at the pool hall. Then someone else said he was waiting in the park near West 78th Street. Another guy said maybe he was at the train station. We went all over New York looking for that guy. Then real late at night we came home. And who do you think was there? Well, it sure wasn't Willy! It was the good old cops.

"They told us to get in the car. We all went over to the East Side around 98th Street. There was a robbery in one of the big apartments. You know, one that looks down on the park. The cops had caught the robbers red-handed. They said two guys were dead already and another guy was going fast. When we got there, cops and dogs were running around all over the place.

"There was some doctor in a white coat with blood on it. He had a flashlight. He and the cops were all around this guy on the sidewalk. Someone told us it was one of the robbers. His

124

gun had gone off in his face. No one could tell who it was. That's when I began to see why the cops wanted us there. They thought it was Willy, but no one could tell anymore.

"I went over and got down by him. Even with his face mostly gone, it was Willy all right. I told him it was me. He moved his head just a little. He reached up and put his arms around me. I was holding him real close to me. Then he says slowly, 'Mike, are you going to miss me? I sure don't want to die!' I said, 'Yes, brother, I am going to miss you. And I love you, man.' He looked up at me and said, 'Mike, I'm sorry' and closed his eyes. Then I heard this sound in his throat like water running. A lot of blood came up . . . and he was gone."

Mike puts his head down. It's a long, long time before he can say any more. Rosa pictures Willy and what his life must have been like. She feels so sad about all of it. How can some people have it so good? But there are others like Willy who have nothing go right. And Mike . . . what a good, true friend he was to Willy. How it must hurt him that he couldn't save Willy in the end.

After a long while, Mike lets go of Rosa and stands up. He walks out on the sidewalk and turns back to face her. He puts his hand on his heart. Then he smiles. "I don't promise nothing, baby," Mike says. The smile goes away. "But after what I saw last night, I think I'm through with fighting. Men like me got to learn to get by without using hands or guns. If we can't, we might just as well keep Willy company." Mike brushes a hand across his eyes. "Don't say nothing, Rosa. Just listen. I really dig your company. I think you know that. But now I want to go and be by myself for a time. OK?"

"OK, Mike." Rosa throws him a slow kiss.

"Thanks for listening," he calls as he heads off. "I'll be back, baby."

"I'll be waiting," Rosa says.

After Mike goes, Rosa puts her arms around her legs. New York, she thinks. What a great big beautiful, hard, sad town this is. And then all the tears Rosa has been holding inside come out. She had to keep from crying so she could be brave for Mike. She puts her head in her hands and lets herself go.

Rosa doesn't see Mike for six days. It has also been six days since Willy died. All week Mike has been by himself, but tonight he's going out. It's Rosa's opening at Street Scene. James has said that just this once he'll give passes to Rosa's friends.

Rosa, Jill, Harriet and Luther are sitting in the club drinking soda. The place is full of people. This is really it, Rosa thinks to herself. She looks around at the faces. Tonight they'll like me only if I'm really good, not because I'm a friend.

"Here comes your boyfriend, Southern."
Luther gives Rosa a push.

"Now stop cutting up, Luther," Jill says.
"Rosa doesn't have time for love."

"Keep quiet, you two," Rosa laughs.

Mike sits down beside Rosa. "Hi, beautiful,"
he says, giving her a kiss.

Rosa smiles at him. "That makes my night,
Mike." Now Rosa sees Ad come in. He walks
through the people to get to Rosa. He sits
down, out of breath.

"Where have you been, Ad?" Rosa asks.

Harriet hands Ad a soda. He takes a drink
before saying, "I was late because I got a
phone call."

Now James is walking up the ramp to give
Rosa's introduction. "Ad," Rosa says, "don't
keep me waiting. I've got to go on. Who was it
from?" Ad has a shiny look in his eyes. "May,"
he tells her, then he stops.

"Ad, cut it out!" Rosa knows he's talking
slowly to kid her.

Ad puts his hand on Rosa's. "May asked how
you're doing, little sister. When I told her about
tonight, she said to give you her love." Ad looks
at Rosa. "She also said she'll be happy to see
you home again for . . ." Here Ad says each
word slowly, "your last—year—in—Burns!"

"Far out, Rosa," Harriet cries.

Luther and Jill throw their arms around Rosa. Mike and Rosa look at one another. Rosa knows just what Mike is thinking. She takes his hand. "Don't look so sad," she tells him under her breath. "I'll be back, baby."

Mike laughs. "And I'll be waiting!" he says.

Rosa looks up to where James is standing. He says, "And now, all the way from Burns, Alabama! Let's hear it for Rosa Essay!"

Rosa's friends are screaming and pounding their feet. Rosa goes up the ramp. James hands her the mike and walks off. Rosa stands with her head down, waiting for quiet. At last it comes. The lights go down. The music starts. Rosa looks toward her friends. But the light on her face is so bright that she can't see.

"I sing this song," Rosa tells the waiting faces, "for a boy who died last week. His life was short and sad. But I think maybe he's happy now. So, Willy, wherever you are, this one is for you . . ." Rosa starts to sing.

"I been doing some hard running,

"But this road is going to end someday,

"Oh, yes, it's going to end someday."

The music comes from Rosa's soul. And she keeps on singing. Nothing will ever stop her now.